Growing Up Different

Sometimes I felt that I never had a mother, that I came out of God knows what. I wonder if that's why I don't want an ordinary life either? Why I like moving around, and stay away from girls at school who talk about wearing their mother's clothes, or going shopping with their mothers, or even having a fight with their mothers.

Once when we were in a housekeeping apartment, in St. Louis, I went into a butcher shop and picked out a steak. I told the butcher I wanted the fat all cut off, and the end chopped for hamburger. He said, "Your mother taught you properly how to buy meat, young lady."

"My mother's been dead for ten years," I said, "so she hasn't taught me anything." The store was full, and the poor women were shocked out of their minds. I stalked out of the store (with the steak) but once outside I burst into tears. It was a bratty thing to do, and I don't know why I did it. It's weird, because there are times when deep down I don't mind so much that I haven't got a mother: this way I don't have to share Lenny with anyone. It's just the two of us.

Just the Two of Us

HILA COLMAN

SCHOLASTIC INC.
New York Toronto London Auckland Sydney Tokyo

ISBN 0-590-32512-4

Copyright © 1984 by Hila Colman. All rights reserved. Published by Scholastic Inc.

12 11 10 9 8 7 6 5 4 3 2 1   8   4 5 6 7 8 9/8

Printed in the U. S. A.   01

For Joel

Chapter One

I was in the bathroom putting green polish on my toenails when Lenny banged on the door. "Come on, Indian. We're buying a restaurant. We gotta meet a real estate agent in twenty minutes."

There's no way you can make nail polish dry in a hurry. That was my fate in life: I was washing my hair when we were in an earthquake in California. I thought all the shaking and dizziness was because my head was down in the sink. Lenny says I'm sure to be in the bathtub when it's time for my wedding. But that was one I didn't think I had to worry about since I couldn't imagine myself married.

I put on my green, open-toed sandals, without stockings (my big toe smeared anyway), and we went to meet the real estate agent. Lenny is my father. He is very good-looking (something like a brooding Burt Reynolds), and women flirt with him all the time, making believe they are enchanted with me, his fourteen-year-old daughter. I am sure most of them wish I'd drop dead, or at least disappear. I could tell them from the beginning that they're wasting their time, because my darling father is still in love with my mother, who died when I was a year old. The most they'll get may be a dinner or two, and then he'll make it clear he doesn't want to get involved. Besides, we're very happy the way we are, just the two of us.

The real estate lady was no different. She had red hair and big blue eyes, and she fluttered her false eyelashes in a way that made me avoid Lenny's eyes. We'd both giggle. But the restaurant was part of an old house, and it was something else. It was at the end of what they call the "common" or "green" in New England towns. It was a big, old-fashioned Victorian house that someone had converted into a restaurant and, on the second floor, an apartment. It was beautiful and I loved it, but it made me nervous. It looked so permanent, so settled, not like any of the rather transient places we had lived in. This house was the kind a person gets born and grows up in, with lots of family — aunts and uncles and grandparents — and Christmas parties and Fourth of July picnics. Lenny and I had always moved around, and besides Lenny, the only family I had were his father and an aunt, my mother's sister. Neither one did much good because I never saw them. It was like pulling teeth to get a word out of Lenny about the past. He shut up like a clam when I asked questions, and when I was old enough to recognize that closed, pained look on his face, I stopped asking.

But I knew this much: Lenny's mother had been killed in an automobile accident when he was seven or eight, and what he wouldn't talk about — but what I figured out — was that he blamed his father and himself for her death. I think his mother had been coming to pick him up from a birthday party when her car was hit, and in his child's mind he felt he shouldn't have been at the party. To add to his pain, he was angry that his father had let his mother drive on that foggy day. Poor Lenny. I think he never forgave his father. When Lenny left home, at sixteen, his father remarried and moved to South America, where his new wife had grown up. Every Christmas I got a card with a five-dollar bill enclosed from a grandfather whose unsmiling, handsome, bearded face I knew only from a picture. Lenny usually grunted when I showed him the card, signed "Your Grandfather, Joseph Thompson," and often made a disparaging remark about the five dollars.

On my mother's side, there's only my Aunt Sheila, who lives in Vancouver. Once, when we were in Seattle, I asked Lenny if we couldn't go to see her, but he said he hadn't talked to her since my mother died and he didn't think we'd be welcome. "When you're a big girl, if you want to get in touch with her you can," he'd said to me. "But she doesn't like me, and I don't like her."

"If she doesn't like you, then I don't like her, either," I remember saying. But sometimes when I was lonesome I thought about her. However, I decided that there must be something wrong with a person who didn't like Lenny.

"Do you like the house? Do you like it?" When Lenny is excited, he says things twice.

"It's okay," I said.

He looked daggers at me and then smiled knowingly. He thought I was playing it cool for the benefit of the red-haired real estate lady. But she was far from my mind. I was worried about Lenny settling down. He had talked for months about wanting to buy a restaurant and live what he called "a normal life." "You're getting to be a young lady," he had said to me, making it sound like the pits. "This moving around is no good. You should have a proper social life."

"If you think I'm going to go to proms with preppies and cheer at football games, think again. I adore living in motels and hotels, and I love saying good-bye. Farewell parties make me feel wanted." I would never in a million years let Lenny know that lately I noticed boys looking at me, and I wondered what it would be like to have a boyfriend. I mean a real boyfriend whom I knew and liked well enough to let kiss me and stuff like that.

It was Lenny who had counted up that we had moved six times in ten years. "That means we hardly stayed anywhere for two years."

"Except in Denver," I told him. "We were there for almost three." He was not impressed. We moved because of the kind of jobs my father had. He's a restaurant whiz: Sometimes he sets up restaurants for a chain of hotels, sometimes he establishes concessions for fast food outfits, once he worked for something called the Big Shrimp (which predictably closed in three months), and another time he was the chef in an elegant French restaurant in Montreal.

Lenny followed Mrs. Babcock (the redhead) around this Victorian house as if he were lord of the manor. "I think I'll panel the walls with pine," he said, walking through the downstairs. "I don't like the wallpaper. The kitchen is too small and will have to be enlarged." Upstairs, he said that there had to be a second bathroom in the apartment.

"Why did you waste that woman's time?" I asked him when we were back in the motel where we'd been staying for the past few weeks.

"What do you mean? I'm buying that place. I'm going to give her a deposit on it tomorrow." He sounded as if he meant it.

"I'm going swimming," I said. We were in one of our classier homes-away-from-home and had adjoining, poolside rooms.

Lenny pulled on his mustache, gave me a what-have-I-done-to-deserve-this look, and went into his own room.

Later, floating on my back in the pool, I could see him stretched on a chaise with a book that he wasn't reading in his hand. I had a lot to think about. I hadn't minded moving around, because I sensed Lenny's restlessness. It wasn't accidental that he took the kind of jobs he did, and when he finished one he went on to the next immediately. I believed that his not wanting to lead a conventional domestic life had a lot to do with my mother and the pain of losing her.

He was very young when he married my mother, Lily. She was eighteen, and he was nineteen. I was born when my mother was twenty. They were very much in love. My father was a short-order cook in a diner in Georgia, and my mother did sewing at home. I still have two exquisite long, white dresses that she made for me — every stitch by hand.

Sometimes he does talk about how happy they were together even though they didn't have much money. He says he really learned how to cook because he had to invent new ways to make cheap meals for them. My mother apparently wasn't big on cooking.

What my father won't talk about is how and why she died. I mean any details. I know a few facts, but that's all: I know she was frail (I could tell that from the few pictures I've seen) and that she got pneumonia and was taken to the hospital. But then she came home, and a week or so later she suddenly died. "Didn't they have penicillin then?" I had asked Lenny.

"Yes, of course, but she was allergic to it. I don't want to talk about it."

"Wasn't there any other antibiotic? Why did they send her home from the hospital if she wasn't all better? Maybe if she'd stayed there. . . ." Lenny didn't let me finish the sentence. His face was white.

"I said I didn't want to talk about it. She's dead. There's nothing we can do about it."

We had that conversation when I was eight years old, and that night Lenny had held me in his arms when he came in to say goodnight and asked me to please understand that there were some things he couldn't talk about. When I was older I would understand. I am older, and I still don't understand. And I don't understand why he gave me only one snapshot of her — a lovely young woman in shorts and a T-shirt — that I have in a silver frame on my dresser, and why he hoards the other pictures and makes up flimsy excuses when I ask to see them. I think he's keeping something from me, and I think about it sometimes when I can't fall asleep. Did she take too many pills and die because of that? I hate that he won't tell me everything about my own mother.

Sometimes I feel that I never had a mother, that I came out of God knows what. I wonder if that's why I don't want an ordinary life, either? Why I like moving around, and why I stay away from girls at school who talk about wearing their mothers' clothes, or going shopping with their mothers, or even having fights with their mothers.

Once when we were in a housekeeping apartment in St. Louis, I went into a butcher shop and picked out a steak. I told the butcher I wanted all the fat cut off and the end chopped for hamburger. He said, "Your mother taught you properly how to buy meat, young lady."

"My mother's been dead for ten years," I said, "so she hasn't taught me anything." The store was full, and the poor women were shocked out of their minds. I stalked out of the store (with the steak), but once outside I burst into tears. It was a bratty thing to do, and I don't know why I did it. It's weird, because there are times when deep down I don't mind so much that I haven't got a mother: This way I don't have to share Lenny with anyone. It's just the two of us.

All the time I was swimming I was trying to figure out why Lenny wanted to buy a restaurant and settle down now. I knew he was doing it partly for me — I'd be going into senior high in another year and Lenny thought it was important to stay put — but I also wondered if he was finally ready to lead a different kind of life. The thought made me nervous. I liked things the way they were, and I wanted them to stay that way between Lenny and me. Did his wanting to settle down in a big house now mean that he was ready to forget about my mother?

When I came out of the pool, Lenny had disappeared into his room. I took a shower and was in my terry-cloth robe when he knocked on the door. "Come in," I told him.

Lenny sat down on a big fake leather chair popular in classy motels. "You do really like the house, don't you?"

"It's very nice." I proceeded to brush my hair, which was wet and long and should have been dried first.

"What's the matter?"

I put down the brush cautiously. "I thought we had a pretty good life the way we were." Suddenly I knew I was scared stiff. Compton Falls, Mass. I had seen enough of the town and the kids on the street to feel that I would never fit in. I was used to cities, where you can walk around the streets and no one looks at you and there are lots of people, shops, and movies. Most of Dad's jobs had been in cities, from New Orleans to San Francisco. A small town scared me. There was nothing I'd ever heard about one that was reassuring: cliques, gossip, everyone knowing everyone else's business, strangers not welcome. Samantha Thompson and her father who owned the new restaurant would be outsiders.

"Listen, Indian," — he called me that because of my straight black hair and my olive skin — "I think it's time you had a real home. And stayed in one place long enough to have friends. Soon you'll be old enough to want to go out on dates and have a social life like other girls your age. I'm not looking forward to it, but I've got to think about those things. I can't keep you to myself forever."

"I'm not interested in what you call a social life. I've been to parties, but — well, I just don't fit in." I didn't remind him of the occasions I had called him to pick me up from a party early with the excuse that I didn't feel well. But Lenny didn't need to be reminded.

"I know all about that," he said. "Of course you didn't fit in. You were always either just coming into a new class or leaving one. That's exactly the point. You're a very pretty and attractive girl — moving around didn't hurt when you were a little kid, but you're getting to be a young lady now and I want you to have a proper life. Besides," he added with a grin, "I'm ready myself to settle down. Don't think I'm doing this just for you."

"Who ever accused you of being noble? Are we going to have dinner here?" The conversation was giving me a headache.

"No, I'm taking you out to celebrate."

Lenny was a fusspot about how I looked, so I got dressed up in heels, a skirt, a frilly blouse, and a neat short velvet jacket he had bought for me. It was a warm June night and I didn't really need the jacket. But the thin blouse showed so much of my figure I was embarrassed. It was moments like that I wished I had a mother to tell me if all girls my age changed so much. But I hadn't yet told Lenny what was really worrying me.

My father didn't have to be in a town more than five minutes before he knew the best, and the most expensive, restaurant around, and broke or not (and sometimes we were), that's where he would head. "Chalk it up to business," he would say. "I have to keep in touch." So I wasn't surprised when he drove to a stone house up in the hills that clearly did not have neon signs on the highway for tourists. It had almost no sign at all, just some discreet lettering next to a mailbox that read THE HARRISON HOUSE. My father must have cased the place before, because when we went inside, the maître d' greeted us with a big, toothy smile and led us to a comfortable round table right near the wood-burning fire with a "Is this all right, Mr. Thompson?"

"Perfect," Lenny said.

After Dad ordered our dinner, having explained carefully to the waiter how he wanted each dish prepared, he settled back in his chair and looked at me. "What's the matter, Indian? You have something on your mind." Lenny doesn't miss much.

"As a matter of fact, I have."

"You feel like talking about it?"

"I don't really, but I suppose this is as good a time as any." I knew I had to get it off my chest, but I didn't know how to say it. Lenny and I have such a funny relationship. I mean, we're as close as any two people can be, yet there are some things we never talk about. Very private things, like he doesn't want to talk about my mother, and I can't talk to him about boys and certain feelings I have. For instance, when I came out of my room that night, he said, "You don't need that jacket; it's very warm."

"I get chilly," I said, "and besides, I like the way it looks." No way could I explain to Lenny that I didn't want my developing figure to show. Yet when I'd been in my bathing suit that same afternoon and some boys had stared at me when they walked past the pool, I'd looked the other way but felt good about my figure. Very complicated things were happening to me — to my body and to my feelings, and both kept changing. Sometimes I felt terrific that I was getting breasts and curves, and I really felt excited when I looked at myself in the mirror. Other times I just felt scared and I wanted to cover myself up in a shapeless sack and hide. I don't know exactly what I was afraid of, except perhaps my own sudden, intense feelings.

Once Dad tried to talk to me about sex. I must have been around eleven or twelve, and I suppose he figured I'd be getting my period sometime along then. Poor Lenny — he wanted so hard to be a mother to me as well as a father. He hemmed and hawed, and asked a few questions, and I let him go on for a bit until I couldn't stand his embarrassment, and I put him out of his misery. I told him, "If you're trying to tell me about where babies come from, don't bother. I know all about it. And if you're worried that once I become a woman, I'm going to mess around with boys, forget it. I have a lot of plans for what I want to do, and having babies is not one of them."

Dad pretended to be shocked that I knew so much, but he was mighty relieved. "I trust you, honey," he said, "but you know I have a very big responsibility bringing up a daughter."

What we never did talk about was Dad's sex life. It was only recently that I started to think about it seriously, probably because of what was happening to me. I had been kissed by boys, and a couple of times a little more than just kissed, but it hadn't been particularly exciting. But lately I'd been more aware of boys and how they looked at me, and a few times I found myself wondering what it would be like to be kissed by a particular boy. It could be someone I didn't even know, just a kid I saw on the street or on TV or in the movies. There was one boy, a regular in a TV show, whom I thought about at night when I couldn't fall asleep. When he looked up from the screen I felt he was looking right at me. One night I was watching his show in my nightgown, and suddenly I wrapped myself in a blanket, I felt so weird and embarrassed.

I'm not exactly dumb about sex, and here was my father — thirty-five years old, handsome, and healthy. Didn't he want a woman in his life? While we had been moving around, he'd occasionally go out with a woman, but I knew it was always something casual, and besides, we never stayed long enough in one place for anything to get serious. The truth is, my father's a bit of a prude: He has a fit if he hears me use a four-letter word, and once in a while when he's caught me running from the bathroom to my bedroom naked, he's bawled me out for having no modesty.

It was only after we'd eaten the oysters casino Dad had ordered that I got around to talking. I'm not one to beat around the bush, so I came right out with what I had to say. "I've been thinking that now that you've bought a house and will have the restaurant, you must be thinking of settling down. Does that mean you're going to want to get married?"

"Oh, my God, is that what's been worrying you? Why should I want to get married? I've got you to take care of me, haven't I?" Lenny sipped his wine. He allowed me one glass.

"I know, but . . . You talk about sending me off to college someday. Then you'd be alone."

That's years away." He laughed. "You trying to fix me up?"

"I wouldn't know anyone to fix you up with. But I don't know. Are you not looking for someone because of me?"

"Heck, no. I like my life the way it is. I was in love with your mother, and maybe that was enough for me. Are you trying to get rid of me or are you dying for a stepmother? Aren't I enough?" He said it with a smile, but his eyes were searching my face.

"You're plenty. I was just thinking of you. I . . . well, I don't want to hamper your style. I'm not a kid anymore; it isn't as if you have to take care of me. I just don't want to be in your way."

"Indian, honey, you'll never be in my way. I don't want another woman; I don't need another woman. So stop worrying your pretty head, will you? And you are pretty. You're the one who's going to be running away from me one of these days."

"You don't have to worry about that," I told him.

We both got busy with our broiled salmon after that, and I was relieved. I honestly don't think I'm a selfish person, but I always thought of Lenny and me together. I couldn't imagine life any other way. I drank my glass of wine and ordered a fantastic chocolate and whipped-cream dessert.

Dad drove home slowly, and I made him drive around the green twice. I wanted to get more of a feel of the place.

"This town sure looks dead," I said. There wasn't a soul on the street, and the houses looked closed up for the night.

"I like it. It's so peaceful."

My father had never looked for anything peaceful before.

"It's peaceful, all right," I told him.

Of course, I didn't know then that my first year in Compton Falls was going to be the least peaceful year of my life.

Chapter Two

Moving. If there is one thing I'm really good at, it's packing and moving. Lord knows I've had experience. The only trouble is, Lenny and I have a completely different approach. I like to go at it slowly and get started days in advance. I'm not the neatest person in the world, but I don't like packing dirty clothes, so I'm washing and ironing like a fiend and collecting tons of tissue paper for days until Lenny looks at my room in disgust and says I'll need a suitcase for each dress.

"Not if you pack them right," I snap back at him, and he laughs and says I sound like someone's mother.

Sometimes I feel like his mother. For a man who can spend an hour fussing over the stove to get a sauce exactly to his taste, it beats me how he can make a jumble of his suits, shirts, underwear, and shoes in twenty minutes and call it packing. He gets furious when I take everything out and do it over.

Moving into Compton Falls Inn (we called it that from the beginning) was no different. Worse, if anything.

This time we had to take a long, hot drive back to Philadelphia, the last place we had lived, to get our few pieces of furniture, books, pictures, etc., from someone's garage, put them into a U-Haul, and drive back to Massachusetts. It was boring. Especially Lenny's refrain at intervals along the way: "Well, Indian, this is the last time we'll be doing this." He made it sound like the end of some terminal disease. As if I wasn't nervous enough.

"Do you think the desk should be downstairs where people can see it, or up in my room?" I asked Lenny. Our jumble of possessions was piled up in the central hall. There wasn't much. Fortunately Dad had bought essentials like beds and a couple of tables and chairs from the previous owner. The restaurant was pretty well equipped with the important appliances, which had been one of its attractions, but Lenny had to change the kitchen and the cabinets to suit himself.

The desk was my most precious piece. It was an heirloom from my mother's family, handed down from mother to daughter, and my mother had inherited it when her mother had died before I was born. It was a beautiful, delicate piece of furniture, made of satinwood, with slender legs and an inlaid, finely marked veneer top. Whenever I sat at it I felt I should be wearing a long gown and using a quill pen.

"You do what you want," Lenny said. He was funny about that desk. He liked me to use it, but at the same time, when I did he worried me crazy about its getting scratched or any of the veneer coming off.

"It would look pretty in this hall. It goes with this house. We could keep a bowl of fresh flowers on it so that people wouldn't use it to put things on."

"Yeah." Lenny was standing in the archway to the big dining room, studying the room and paying no attention. I pushed the desk to the center of the wall, and fished a dark red bowl out of one of the cartons. It looked pretty even in the middle of the mess, and I made a mental note to get some flowers when I went shopping.

I was used to being in a strange town, but this time it was different. I was going to be *living* here. I tried not to stare at the girls I saw in the post office and around the village, but I was wildly curious. If they noticed me at all they probably thought I was a summer visitor, but I knew that some of them (those that looked my age) might later be my classmates, and maybe even my friends someday. But no one did notice me. Except once a boy almost hit me with his bike while I was crossing the street and said quite rudely, "Watch where you're going."

"*You* watch," I called after him but he didn't turn around.

My memory of that summer is one of living in a God-awful mess. My usual summer routine of sleeping until ten or eleven in the morning was ruined by carpenters, plumbers, and painters arriving every day at eight and starting the racket. Besides, I did want to be helpful. Most days Lenny would have been up for hours even at eight when I sleepily made my way downstairs in search of breakfast and stumbled over piles of lumber, buckets of paint, or a stove or sink in the middle of the hall. Sardines and a glass of milk were the easiest, and Lenny said I ate enough Norwegian sardines that summer to change the import-export ratio of the United States.

I spent a lot of time taking dishes out of cabinets, washing them, and eventually putting them back. I only broke two. I ran errands. I watched pieces of wood be miraculously fitted together and turned into cabinets. I learned about two-by-fours, and tongue and groove, and what a smidgen of ochre can do to the color of paint. I spent a lot of time shopping with Lenny for small appliances and special utensils, looking for local sources for fresh eggs and chickens, and for vegetables and meats. I lolled around and sun-bathed and worried about what was going to happen.

I felt uneasy. Lenny was very preoccupied. I could see already that the restaurant was going to be different from a job. Lenny had a new baby that was going to demand a lot of his loving care and attention. Even at night, after the workmen had gone home, he'd sit with one of those big yellow pads, figuring and planning. I couldn't even get him to watch reruns of *M*A*S*H*, our favorite TV show.

Very often I went for a walk late in the afternoon.

At our end of the green there was a road that took you immediately out of the village into the country. First you walked past a cemetery (no more dead than the rest of the town) and then along a road that went up into the hills. The further you walked the fewer houses there were. I didn't mind that kind of quiet. In a city where there are people there should be noise and movement, but quiet in the country is different. It belongs. One day in August I walked further than usual and came to a nursery. There was a greenhouse, rows of plantings, and a tiny red house set against a hill. The house looked cozy and I could see a small plaque that showed it was built in 1790. A woman was squatting on the ground working among trays of small plants set out for display.

That was my first sight of Liz Barnes: a dirt-streaked face, and grubby hands putting some evil-smelling stuff (manure?) into the earth.

She smiled at me as if she knew me. It was the friendliest greeting I'd had yet in Compton Falls. "Hi," she called out.

"Hi." I walked over to her and admired her flowers.

"I'm glad to see someone walking. People around here consider a car the only means of transportation." She was hot and sweaty and she wasn't exactly pretty, but she had a healthy, earthy look about her. Her eyes were disconcertingly direct and very blue against her tanned face. "I bet you're a city girl. City people walk a lot more than country people, did you know that?"

"I thought city people rode around in limousines," I said. She thought that was a funny remark. Her face crinkled up when she laughed.

I asked her about flowers, and she took me into the greenhouse and sold me a plant to put into the red bowl. She said that was more sensible than cut flowers, and offered to drop it off when she went by later so that I wouldn't have to carry it home. "I'm glad someone bought that place," she said. "It was going to pot, empty. I'd love to get my hands on the grounds. At one time it was beautiful, but it's a mess now. I'm not trying to drum up business," she added with her sudden smile. "I have more than I can do, but I always liked that place."

"I think we should do some landscaping. I'll ask my father."

Lenny and I were sitting in back of the house, Lenny with a drink in his hand and me with a glass of tomato juice, when I got around to telling him about the nursery. "She said this place used to be beautiful," I said, looking at what was once probably a lovely lawn but was now a lot of scrubby grass. The land itself was naturally pretty, sloping down to a tiny stream and a clump of pine and birch trees. Along the way a few sad flowering bushes were the remaining signs that once someone had cared.

"We'll have to let it go for now," Lenny said. "Let's get the house fixed up first. The outdoors can wait until spring."

"I suppose so, but it looks awful." A good deal of the restaurant looked out to the back of the house. "Maybe the flower lady can suggest something to make it look a little better so people won't have to look at this while they're eating."

We were still sitting there when Liz Barnes drove up. She had washed her face and brushed her hair, but she hadn't changed from her streaked jeans and faded T-shirt. I could see she wasn't the kind who would flutter her eyes at Lenny, and he immediately looked bored. He would be, with a woman who didn't bother about the way she looked, and it was soon obvious my new friend was not making a hit.

Lenny turned up his nose at every suggestion she made. No, he didn't want the lawn seeded and fertilized now, although she said that was the only way he would have a lawn in the spring. He was not interested when she suggested that if we put in some bulbs in the fall, we'd have something pretty in the spring — "You can plant them yourselves," she added. "They don't cost much, and I wouldn't mind preparing the ground. . . ."

We walked around the grounds, and after making a few more suggestions, she gave up gracefully if a little coldly. "I don't want to waste your time, Mr. Thompson. I'll get your plant from the car," she said to me. "Good evening."

The plant looked gorgeous in the red bowl. "You weren't very nice to her," I said to Lenny. He was broiling a Delmonico steak for our dinner.

"Her hands and feet were grubby," he remarked.

"For Pete's sake, you turkey, she works with dirt. What'd you expect, someone who just stepped out of a beauty parlor?"

"I'm going to make this really rare, is that okay?" All innocent-looking and smiling. Oh, boy.

In an indirect way it was because of Liz that I met Josh. Josh Smiley. Some days are good and some are bad, and that day was awful. Cool Lenny was in a rage in the morning because the carpenter had put the shelves in wrong in the pantry. They had to be ripped out and Lenny was carrying on that we wouldn't be ready to open on time. A proof of an ad in the newspaper came in with a word misspelled and I was sneezing my head off from some darn pollen in the air.

When I went for my walk in the afternoon, on the spur of the moment I decided to buy a bunch of bulbs with my own money. I needed something to cheer me up. So I stopped at the nursery. Liz Barnes was pretty cool, for which I could hardly blame her. "Your father said he didn't want any," she said to me. We were in the greenhouse, and her hands were as grubby as the other day.

"I'm buying them. I'll plant them myself."

She gave me an amused smile, the kind that I saw in her eyes a lot of the time. As if she thought the world was pretty funny. "Won't that offend your father?"

"Oh, no." I laughed. "He won't mind. I thought they'd cheer me up. Give me something to do."

"It must be lonesome for you, coming into a new town and not having any friends." She looked sympathetic. "When school opens it will be different." She put the bulbs in a box and handed them to me. "Be careful they don't fall out the bottom — it's not a very good carton, but it's all I've got. Plant them about six inches apart and not too deep. I hope they do cheer you up."

"I'm okay. I'm used to not having many friends. My father and I get along fine." She gave me that funny smile again, as if she was thinking, *I'd like to believe you, but. . . .* She was neat, that flower lady.

I was walking up the hill from the nursery

to our house, when of course the bottom fell out of the soggy carton, and all the bulbs and the dirt with them plopped to the ground. I squatted on the road to gather them up, but what was I going to put them in? The only thing I could think of was to take off my slip, thanking my good luck I was wearing one that had straps I could undo. It had been a hot day, too hot for jeans. I didn't see anyone coming and I was wiggling out of my white cotton slip when a boy on a bike came whizzing around the curve of the hill. In a panic I sat down with the darn slip half around my legs and half under my skirt.

"Want some help?" He pulled over and stopped his bike. It was the boy who had almost knocked me down before.

"No thanks."

He glanced at the broken carton and the bulbs, and it wasn't hard to figure out what had happened. "I could put your bulbs in my basket and take them home for you."

"I can manage, thank you."

He shrugged and got back on his bike. I stood up, and my slip fell down around my ankles exactly when he turned around to wave good-bye.

With as much dignity as possible I stepped out of my slip, and then we both broke into hysterical giggles.

"Okay, you win." I gathered up the bulbs and deposited them in his wire basket. "I live the other side of the hill. The old restaurant."

"I know where you live," he said. "I'll wait for you there." And he took off.

How did he know where I lived? I wondered. Small town, of course — everyone knowing about everybody. Yuck.

He was waiting in front of the house when I got there. "I'll get a bag," I said and ran inside and came back with a brown paper grocery bag.

"Do you think I could have a glass of water?" He had brown, curly hair, lots of it, and a nice face.

I hesitated a few seconds, I guess too long. "Never mind," he said. "I can wait till I get home."

"No, come on in." He followed me into the kitchen.

"You almost knocked me over with your bike awhile back," I said. "You want ice?"

"No thanks. I'm sorry about that, but I wouldn't have hit you."

"It was real close."

"I said I'm sorry."

Dad was standing in the doorway looking at us. He put out his hand to Josh. "I'm Lenny Thompson, Samantha's father."

Josh introduced himself, and they shook hands. Immediately my father became The Genial Host. And I mean in capital letters, graciously acting like he'd been waiting all summer to have a charming boy like Josh drop in so he could show off his new restaurant to him. You'd think Josh would be spending a mint there the way Lenny led him around, pointing out all the new gadgets in the kitchen, the choppers and mixers, the special lights, the wine closet, and the cabinets that turned around, Lenny's favorite toy. He had Josh eating out of his hand. I could have killed him. I didn't want Lenny to make friends for me. I said quite loudly that I had a lot of things to do, and Josh left.

"He seems like a nice boy," Lenny said. "Where'd you meet him?"

"How do you know he's nice? You don't even know him."

"I said he *seems.* My, you're touchy. You didn't tell me where you met."

"He picked me up on the road. I bought some bulbs and dropped them. But I've seen him around the village."

Lenny had the kind of smile on his face that meant he was laughing at me. "You didn't sound very cordial after he did you a favor."

I caught Lenny's eye and knew he was laughing at me. "You're blushing," he said, laughing out loud.

"Go jump in the lake, you turkey." I threw a wad of paper napkins at him. "You weren't so cordial when the flower lady was here," I called after him, "so you're no one to talk."

Chapter Three

Did I say Lenny doesn't get excited about big things? I was wrong. He was nervous as a cat the day the restaurant was to open. It was the Thursday before Labor Day weekend. His plan was to start off being open on Thursday, Friday, Saturday, and Sunday nights for dinner and then see later if he wanted to add lunches and a Sunday brunch. He had hired an assistant cook to do salads and desserts, under his supervision. Lenny made all the entrees himself. Ralph was a big, sad-faced Italian, who later told me his father was in jail for having beat up his mother. Ralph's nephew, Jerry, was a kitchen helper. Two women from the village, Mary and Lena Miano, were hired to wait on tables. Lenny told me if I wanted I could take people's coats in the hall and look pretty.

Dad didn't believe in a big menu. He felt that the choice of a few dishes was ample, but that those dishes had to be very elegant.

He didn't have a full liquor license, but we could serve beer and wine. My father was a nut for elegance: white tablecloths, china dishes, stemmed glasses. "When people go out for dinner," he said, "it's party time. Everyone's a VIP." He fumed for two days because the fire chief said no to using candles in an old frame house.

Opening day, he looked around the dining room and let out a moan. "My God, I forgot flowers. Indian, you gotta go out and get some flowers."

"Where can I get them? There's no florist in Compton Falls."

"What about that woman with the nursery you call the flower lady?"

"The name fits her, but she hasn't got cut flowers. She only has plants."

"Well let her cut some flowers off her plants. Go ahead, get something."

I thought a lot of things I didn't say. Like, 'If you had been nicer to her it would be a little easier to ask favors.' But my frenetic dad was in no mood for any criticism from me. I was less than ecstatic about walking up to the nursery (and how was I supposed to bring enough flowers back with me?) but in a way it was a relief to get out of the house. Lenny, usually quiet-voiced, had shouted at Ralph a few times already, and Ralph, with a chopping knife in his hand, had, without lifting his eyes, told my father what he thought of a fellow cook who told him what to do. "Don't tell me to go easy on the garlic," Ralph said tensely. "I been making salads since before you was born."

It was a warm, sultry day and I thought if it was going to storm I hoped it would before dinner time. We had had quite a few reservations, and I didn't want to be around Lenny if they were canceled.

Miss Barnes was in the greenhouse, and of course she told me what I already knew. "I don't have cut flowers," she said.

"That's what I told my father." I stood there looking helpless, hoping that one of us would get a bright idea. She went on with her work, taking cuttings from large plants and putting them into small pots. I watched.

"I suppose I could cut some flowers from my own garden," she said after a while. "I don't know if they're the kind your father had in mind. They're not like what you'd get at a florist. Mostly marigolds and zinnias and a few chrysanthemums. Very ordinary flowers."

"I think he'd love them," I told her.

She gave me a look that made it clear her impression of my father was that he was a dimwit who couldn't appreciate a flower unless it came out of a box. I didn't think it was the right time to defend him. Meekly, I followed her out to the yard. She had quite a garden in back of her house — rows and rows of vegetables as well as flowers. Suddenly I felt an odd pang of envy: She was so at home with herself and her surroundings. Like she had lived there forever and belonged. For the first time in a long time I wondered what my life might have been like if I'd had a mother and a home, and we hadn't kept moving all the time.

The hazy blue hills behind her house, the brilliant yellow and orange flowers, the marigolds with their special musky odor, and the stillness of the air — all of it gave me a strange feeling, as if I'd been there before or I had known it all in some earlier time. Even the odd yearning that shook me did not surprise me, a yearning for something beyond my life as I knew it. . . .

"You're daydreaming," she said, handing me a bunch of brown and yellow marigolds. "Here, hold these. I'll get some more."

She ended up with more than I could possibly carry. "I'll drive you home," she said in her crisp, matter-of-fact way. I'd never known anyone like her before. Like there were no ifs, buts, or maybes in her vocabulary. She knew exactly what she wanted to do and she did it. I wondered if I would ever grow up to be like that. Sometimes it takes me twenty minutes in front of the mirror to decide whether to wear my hair pulled behind my ears or leave it loose, around my face.

"Would you like to come in?" I asked when we pulled up in front of the house.

"No, thanks." She gave me her amused smile. "I'm sure your father must be very busy today. Lots of luck."

I thanked her profusely for the flowers and

took them inside. I took my time arranging them, and then placed the small vases on each table and bowls of flowers on the mantle and in the hall of the front entrance.

"They look pretty, don't they?" I was showing off to Lenny.

"How much were they?"

"Oh, my. I didn't pay for them. They came from her own garden. . . ."

"She's in business, honey. You can call her up and I'll send her a check."

"I don't think she'd want to be paid for them. I think she was doing us a favor. I have a feeling she'd be insulted."

Lenny gave me a funny stare. "She has a nursery, doesn't she? So flowers are her business. I wouldn't expect someone to come in here and want a meal for nothing. Never mind — I'll take care of it."

I still felt Lenny was making a mistake, but I didn't say anything more.

I went into the kitchen to see if I could be useful, but I could see Ralph didn't want anyone around besides Jerry, who was working at peeling a large bowl of potatoes. Lenny was walking around, moving a chair one place, adjusting glasses at a table, going in and out of the kitchen, and altogether revealing a state of nervous excitement that warned me to stay clear of him.

Up in my own room I had that feeling of being on the threshold of something again, only this time it wasn't so pleasant. I felt a sense of loss, of being left out, and then I realized of course it was Lenny and the restaurant. The feeling I had had in the beginning, when Lenny was getting the place ready. When he had had a job we had been together when he came home. Even if I was doing my homework and he was reading, I felt safe and cozy having him close by.

Lenny had always been there for me. I remember the first day he had taken me to nursery school. I had screamed my head off because I didn't want to go. I wanted to stay with him. The teacher had tried to get me to play with the other children, but I had clung to Lenny's hand and I wouldn't be pried loose. The first three days I was there he stayed with me all day. The kids laughed at Lenny sitting in one of the little chairs, but I didn't care, and Lenny played in the sandbox with me and even went down the slide.

We had a ritual of his reading to me every night or just sitting on my bed and the two of us making up stories together. When he worked crazy hours and I had a babysitter, he'd wake me up, sometimes at midnight, and bring me a cup of hot chocolate and talk to me for a while until I fell asleep again. He was a fantastic father. He never let any of the women who took care of me take me to buy clothes — he always did it, and he let me pick out what I wanted. Even wacky things, like once when I was six or seven I wanted a wedding dress and a veil I saw in a window. We went into the shop and Lenny bought me the veil for when I dressed up for make-believe. A real bride's veil. I remember wearing it until it was in shreds.

But now he was preoccupied, involved in something without me, and I was frightened. It was stupid to be jealous of a restaurant — I mean, that was truly cuckoo — but I had a sudden wild desire to be back in Miss Barnes's garden, as if in that quiet place I could discover an answer to all the mixed-up feelings I was having.

Guests started to come around six o'clock. Lenny had managed to get out of the kitchen in time to greet them in the hall, looking elegant in a dark suit, a blue shirt, and a striped tie. Since it was a stuffy night, there weren't any coats to take, but Lenny wanted me around. I felt kind of silly, but I stayed in the hall with him while he introduced me. I felt terribly proud hearing people's comments as they arrived: "How lovely. . . . You've done wonders with this old house. . . . Such a charming dining room. . . ." Lenny was beaming. I marveled at the way he could do a quick change from being a chef to being a host. There was no sign he'd been sweating in the kitchen all day. I was glad I was his daughter. I mean, I'd always been proud of Lenny, but listening to all the compliments he got that night, suddenly I saw him as a separate person, not just my father. I was hit by the fact that being my father was only a part of his life. It came as a weird shock that evening, watching him greet his guests in his new restaurant, realizing that being a father was only one side of him.

Around seven-thirty, a tall, handsome, gray-haired man appeared with a group. His name was Mr. Swanson. He had a reservation for six, three men and three women; one of them was Liz Barnes. I was knocked over. She looked stunning. She wore a blue dress the color of her eyes, cut low showing her tan, and high heels. Her hair was piled on top of her head, and she had on long, gold earrings. She was a different person. Lenny didn't bat an eye. He greeted them as cordially as he did everyone else and showed them to their table.

Yet I noticed that when he came back through the hall, before showing them the wine list, he stopped in front of the mirror to straighten his tie and smooth his hair. Maybe it was ESP, I don't know, but I had a very distinct feeling that Liz Barnes had an effect on my father — but I wasn't sure if that was good or bad news.

But since so much happened during the evening, that moment was lost in the excitement. The dining room was almost full. More people had come in late, and although Dad had been worried about the early diners not leaving, it was working out pretty well. I don't know if the crowd was typical of Compton Falls, but it was a mixed-up group. Liz Barnes's friends were chic and elegant; there were a few families out for a treat; one very young couple who looked like kids;

and a large group of businessmen (I decided) and their wives, who were making a lot of noise. "They had their drinks before they came here," Dad said.

Mary was bringing in a big tray of food for the business group when we heard a terrific clap of thunder. I saw lightning flash across the windows, and the whole place was plunged into darkness. One woman let out a low scream. Then a man's voice said, "Don't worry; the power'll be back in a few minutes."

Then there was a crash, and I knew Mary's tray had smashed to the floor.

Ralph came running in from the kitchen. "Got any candles, boss?"

Dad had lit a match, and his face looked grim in the flickering light. In seconds the match went out. It was the blackest black I'd ever seen. There wasn't a light outside the house or in it. I stood close by Lenny. It was scary. "There isn't a candle in the house," he said in a quiet voice to Ralph, but I think the whole dining room heard.

"Perhaps you could call the power company, Mr. Thompson, and find out if it is to be a few minutes or a long wait." Liz Barnes's voice was soft but clear.

"Good idea," came from somewhere.

Dad felt his way to the phone, with me close by, but the line was busy. By this time Lenny had pulled himself together, and he went back into the dining room. "I thought I'd remembered everything," he said, facing the dining room, "but I hope you can forgive a city slicker for forgetting the tricks of your New England weather. I'm willing to laugh if you are, and I can only hope that I'll be able to live down this grand opening. I hadn't planned on it being quite so dramatic."

There was some laughter, and then someone applauded and everyone seemed to join in. Dad tried the power company again, but apparently everyone else in Compton Falls was trying to get them, too. Then Liz spoke again, and I think she stood up. "I have lots of candles at my house. I'll get them."

There was a lot of confusion. Mary was crying, matches were being lit and going out. I heard Mr. Swanson say that he'd drive Liz to her house to get candles, but it was Lenny who went out with her. "Bring out wine for everyone," he said to Ralph as he was leaving. "Thank God we have a gas stove."

Actually the evening turned into a lot of fun. Ralph and Jerry produced a couple of flashlights, and some of the men got others from their cars. Mary quieted down, and she and Lena and I got a fire going in the fireplace. Liz and Dad came back with lots of candles and two hurricane lamps. The dining room looked beautiful and romantic, and exactly at 11:46, when the last customer had left, and Dad and Mary and Lena and I were deciding whether to try to clean up, the lights came on.

"Wouldn't you know it," Lenny said, shaking his head and pouring himself a shot of whiskey. "Some timing. Let's just clean up the worst of the mess and do the rest in the morning," he said to the women.

After we got a little order in the kitchen and the two women went home, promising to be back at nine in the morning, Lenny and I sat down.

"What a night," Lenny said. Neither one of us had eaten, so Dad heated some fantastic soup he had made, and we each had a big bowl.

"Lucky Liz Barnes was here," I said. "She was terrific."

"Yeah, she was okay."

I gave my darling father a disgusted look. "She was fantastic. What's the matter with you, anyway? What have you got against her? She's saved you twice now, first with the flowers and tonight with the candles. I should think you'd be grateful."

Lenny tried to look apologetic, in a mocking way. "I'm very grateful. She's a very nice lady, but I'm wondering why you're pushing Liz Barnes?"

"I'm not. Besides, she seems to have a boyfriend. He's very good-looking, too. Distinguished."

"A good twenty years older than she is," Dad said. "He's her lawyer."

"How do you know?"

"She told me."

"Oh." There was a dead silence. I wondered what else they had talked about. "What else did you find out about her?" I finally asked.

"She's never been married, she's thirty-three years old, she's had the nursery for six years, and she loves living alone. She bakes her own bread and adores movies. Anything else you want to know?"

"You found out a lot in a short time." I glanced at Lenny. His eyes were sparkling, and he had a mischievous grin.

"She said she thinks you're going to have a very good time once school opens. She thinks you're very attractive, and you'll make a lot of friends."

"Well, bully for her. Maybe I don't want to make a lot of friends." All of a sudden I hated the idea of Lenny and Liz Barnes talking about me. Who did she think she was?

Dad looked at me in surprise. "I thought you were crazy about her."

"I'll quote you, she's okay." I didn't want to talk about Liz Barnes any more. But when I went up to my room I kept thinking about her. I thought about her working in her garden and how serene she always looked. If opposites attract each other, she and Lenny would make the perfect pair, him being so restless and Liz so cool and peaceful. . . .

Whatever put that in my head? I brushed my hair furiously. She sure had kept her cool that evening, and her hands weren't grubby. I had caught Lenny glancing at her pale pink nail polish more than once, and the rest of her, too.

I turned out my light and got into bed, but I stayed wide-awake. I was jealous: Smart Samantha Thompson was jealous of a perfectly nice lady because she had the decency to be very nice to her father. Oh, boy. I wished she had fat ankles and was cross-eyed. But she didn't, and she wasn't. She was a very attractive woman; I liked her, and I wished she lived a hundred miles away instead of just down the road.

I was a crazy, split-personality. How can you like someone and wish she'd disappear at the same time? It took me hours to fall asleep.

Chapter Four

School opened two days after Labor Day and I had my usual case of nerves about going into a new school. Lenny said I should be used to it by this time, but actually this time was worse because I was going to be staying here.

Ralph said, "Don't worry, Miss Samantha. You'll make many friends." I was in the kitchen watching him make one of his fantastic desserts. There was something amusing about his long, mournful face under his chef's hat, solemnly tasting a light, frothy concoction. He hardly ever smiled, but I felt a warmth from him that came from somewhere deep inside.

"I don't make friends easily." The closest friend I'd ever had was a French exchange student in Chicago. Her name was Ilena, and she was in America for a year along with a brother who was two years older than she. They went everywhere together. We became friends because we both felt the same way.

She expressed my feelings perfectly: "I don't want to get close to someone and then have to say good-bye. Besides, I have my brother; we do things together and then we can talk about them later when we get home." That was just the way I felt about my father, I had told her. She had a wonderful laugh, and she had laughed then and said, "Your father, he is just like a brother to you."

"You don't need many friends," Ralph said in his solemn way, while he rolled out some pastry dough. "A few good friends, that's all anyone needs."

The first day of school I woke up with a stomachache. A real stomachache, and I didn't care whether it came from nerves or not, it was there. But I didn't dare tell Lenny. He would laugh and say I was faking. Maybe it was all in my head, but if it hurt, what difference did that make?

"No, I don't want any breakfast." Lenny look worried. "I'm never hungry the first day of a new school," I said glumly.

I was outside waiting for the bus, which I had been told would pick me up at five minutes after eight, when Josh came along on his bike. "Come on, I'll ride you to school," he said.

"On your bike?" I was astonished.

"Sure, why not? Climb on the bar and hang on." I was dubious.

"I'll fall off."

"Come on, try it."

"Okay." I got on in front of him, sitting

kind of sidesaddle on the bar. We rode for about two minutes, and of course I fell off. I sat in the road and looked up at him.

He was trying not to laugh. "I'm getting used to seeing you that way." He got off the bike and pulled me up. "I'll leave the bike at your house, and we'll walk."

"I could go on the bus." I could see it coming down the road.

"I know. I thought this would be nicer."

"Yeah." It was nice of him to come get me so I wouldn't be going in alone, but I didn't know how to tell him so. The trouble with me is I know how to talk to grown-ups better than I do to kids my own age. I was going into tenth grade and he was in the eleventh, but Josh thought we might be in some classes together. I let him do the talking, especially since my stomach was still fluttery.

"I'm trying to get a group together," he said. "I play the sax and I have a friend who plays an electric guitar. We need a piano and a drummer. Do you play anything?"

"No, I don't. I listen a lot but I don't play. Do you want to go out and play for money?"

"Sure, if we can. And at parties just for ourselves, too. We played whenever we could when there were four of us, but our drummer left for college, and my friend who played the piano moved away. She was very good; she could pick up anything by ear."

"You must miss her," I glanced at him to see his expression, but he didn't register anything.

"Yeah, I do. We were good friends."

I liked the way he said that. I liked a boy who could be friends with a girl without getting silly about it, yet at the same time I wondered if he had a real girl friend. I wished that he didn't. It was weird of me, I know, but if he didn't have anyone, then maybe. . . . I felt him looking at me and there was something in his eyes that made me glance away. I started to run, and he ran with me. Nothing had happened and yet when we reached the school, breathless and laughing, I felt relieved. As if, for the moment at least, I had gotten back on safe ground with Josh.

The school was a pretty, red brick building set back from the road, with a wide lawn in front. I was surprised to see all the cars that drove in. "The kids around here must be rich," I said to Josh.

"So-so. The school is for three towns, so a lot of kids come in their cars. And the teachers all drive."

It was a madhouse inside, everyone trying to find their homeroom. Josh took me to mine and when he left me I felt abandoned. It was awful. I came close to walking out a dozen times. I sat down at a desk, and a couple of girls stared at me, and one even half smiled, but not a soul came over to talk to me. They were too busy catching up with their friends, throwing their arms around each other, and some were so gushy it made me sick: "Oh, darling, I missed you . . . had the most fantastic summer . . . there was this boy in Maine . . . I have a fabulous new stereo . . . you look terrific, you must have lost twenty pounds . . . Candy's having a party...."

My homeroom teacher seemed okay, youngish with a beard—Mr. Worden, also teacher of English lit. But I went from one class to another hating every minute of it, my worst expectations fulfilled. They *were* cliquey. They didn't care about strangers. Everything I had feared was true, and I made up my mind that first day that I was going to be just as aloof as they were. I had gotten along so far without close friends or belonging to a group, and I could go on doing it. I had Lenny, and I would bet anything that none of these kids had a father who was so much fun.

At lunchtime in the cafeteria I didn't see Josh and there was no table where I could sit by myself. "Do you mind if I sit here?" I went over to a table where there were three girls who had been in most of my classes.

"Sure." They introduced themselves as Sharon, Teddi, and Marianne, and I introduced myself. They were polite enough, but I could see that my joining them had squashed whatever conversation they'd been having. I couldn't really hold that against them since I was a stranger, but it was awkward. Sharon made an attempt at conversation with me. "Your father bought the old restaurant, didn't he?"

"Yes, the one on Hill Road."

"It must be fun living in a restaurant," Teddi said. "Do you eat all the time?"

"No, the truth is when you see so much food, you lose your appetite."

"There's a jinx on that place. The last two restaurants went out of business. They failed." Marianne said it with some satisfaction.

"That's cheerful news," I said a little too amiably, but my sarcasm went right past her.

"My father said it was a poor location for a restaurant," she continued.

"Let's hope he's wrong." I gave her a bright smile, and would have happily pushed her smug face into her mashed potatoes.

I got up to leave as quickly as I could, and I was sure they had a great time talking about me the minute my back was turned. I got through the rest of the day okay, but I was more angry than anything when I met Josh outside after school. "How'd it go?" he asked me. He had to walk to my house to pick up his bike.

"I hate it. I'd heard small towns were pretty bad, but this is the worst. Pitsville."

"Wow. You've decided that pretty quickly. Anything special happen?"

"Just a lot of stuck-up kids. I really don't want to talk about it. I'll say things I shouldn't."

"Give us a chance. Maybe you're the one who's stuck-up." He glanced down at me. He's almost a head taller than I am.

"Maybe I am."

Then he gave me that warm grin of his. "You don't mean that. Give us a break, Sammy. You want to have a good time living here, don't you?"

"I'm not counting on it." I still felt sulky from that day.

"It's going to be up to you," he said.

"Thanks." I avoided meeting his eyes. I didn't know how to behave with him. I knew there was something between us, but I didn't know if he wanted to be pal-friends, or if he had something else in mind. In spite of all the places I'd been, I felt that I knew so little. I didn't know my own feelings and I needed to get a cue from him, but he didn't say anything more and got on his bike to take off. I watched him go. He gave me a long look before he left, and I was sure he was going to say something. He waved good-bye, but all he said was "Don't make up your mind about everything the first day, Sammy."

He took off and left me feeling peculiarly uneasy. Like looking at a lousy picture of myself and hoping I didn't look that way.

I found Lenny in the kitchen and was so relieved to see his affectionate, smiling face, I threw my arms around him. "Hey, Indian, you okay?" He hugged me and then held me off to study my face.

"Yeah, I suppose so."

"Did you have a bad day?"

"Terrible. I hate this place." I burst into tears and ran upstairs to my room. I could hear Lenny running up the stairs after me.

"What happened, honey? Tell me." Lenny was walking around my room nervously, the way he does when he's worried. I was too big to cuddle up to him the way I used to when I was little, but I have to confess that's all I wanted. I would have much preferred that to talking.

"Nothing happened really. Except at lunch some girls told me that the restaurant's bound to fail. They as much as said this place had a hex on it. They were so gleeful about it. But it wasn't only that, it was the whole atmosphere. Isn't there any other school I could go to?"

"I'm afraid not. Don't pay any attention to them. They're just jealous because you're pretty and you're smart. They'll come around wanting to be your friends, you wait and see."

"I don't want them for my friends. They're a stuck-up, small-town bunch. I hate them."

Lenny smiled at me. "You know what, you sound like a teenager. Listen, I've got an idea. Why don't you go talk to your friend Liz Barnes, the lady at the nursery? She seems like a sensible dame."

I stared at Lenny in astonishment. "Why should I talk to her?"

He seemed to go into a trance for a moment. He was thinking real hard. "I think talking to a woman could be a help. I know it's not easy coming into a new school and a new town. She's been here for a while, and she's been through it, coming here alone and setting up a business. She's quite a dame. She'd been living in the city, in Brooklyn, taking care of her father. When he died, he left a little money, and she just moved out. Just like that and bought her place here and started the nursery." He gestured with his hands. "You know . . . a woman like Liz could be smarter about these things than I could."

"Is something going on between you and Liz Barnes?" I asked bluntly.

Lenny laughed. "Indian, you know me better than that. I just thought it would be good for you to have a woman like her you could talk to . . . to help you over the rough spots here."

Quickly I went over in my mind if there was any time he could have seen her between the Thursday night when the restaurant opened and today, my first day at school. There wasn't. Over the Labor Day weekend I knew where he was all the time, and he was certainly more than busy with the restaurant.

"Have you seen her lately?" I asked, hoping I didn't sound too inquisitive or suspicious.

"As a matter of fact, she dropped in today to pick up her candleholders. It was lunchtime so I gave her a cup of soup and a sandwich." Lenny picked up a paperweight from my desk and was examining it like it was Elizabeth Taylor's famous diamond. She sure picked her timing. *My first day at school,* I thought. "I think she'll make a good neighbor," he said casually.

I gave him a swift glance. "I thought you treasured your privacy." But then I added quickly, "Anyway, don't worry about me. I can take care of myself."

After he left, I had the distinct feeling that for the first time, Lenny wasn't leveling with me, that he was holding back. This was Wednesday when the restaurant was closed; Ralph and Jerry and the two women wouldn't have been here. He and Liz had had lunch alone — had he fallen in love? Would he fall in love so quickly? What had happened at their lunch?

I was miserable.

I knelt down by the window and looked out at the hills behind the houses. I had thought them beautiful, but now they looked cold and hostile. I felt frightened. I had an absolute conviction that coming to Compton Falls was going to change my life in a terrible way — that everything that had made me feel safe and secure was going to be taken from me.

I was afraid of losing Lenny. I had felt a hint of it the night the restaurant opened when I had seen Lenny as someone apart from being my father: a man with an interest and commitment to a life besides me. I realized he had been trying to tell me something when he bought this place. He was preparing for a life without me, for something for himself when I was grown up and, supposedly, married. And surely that would include a wife for himself.

I buried my face in my arms to shut out the view. I wanted to run back to Lenny to have him tell me that it wasn't going to be like that. I would never leave him for anyone, and he must promise me the same. Of course I didn't. Why shouldn't he fall in love? I was only a kid, a daughter, not a wife. I had never thought of Lenny as being lonely, but there must have been hundreds of times when he'd wanted grown-up love.

I thought about the way Josh had looked at me, and my own confused feelings. Maybe I wasn't such a kid anymore and I wanted something more, too. That really scared me. I didn't want everything to change. I wanted Lenny to stay the same and for me to stay the same. I didn't want to have all these funny feelings; I wished that both Josh and Liz Barnes would disappear and leave us alone. Lenny and I had been happy by ourselves.

The notion that Liz Barnes's pretty garden could have offered me a haven, could have been a place where questions might have found answers, seemed as silly now as believing my life could go on as it had been.

I held my arms tight around myself, feeling that if I didn't, my body might fall into fragments. And suddenly, right out of the blue, I was crying for a mother I had never known.

Chapter Five

The second day of school wasn't much better than the first, nor the third or fourth, either, for that matter. The only person I felt any connection with was Josh, and I didn't know what to do about him. I had never had a real boyfriend, and when I wasn't with Josh I thought about him a lot; that is, when I was alone. But when he stopped in with me after school, as he sometimes did, and Lenny was there, I felt peculiar. Like I didn't like Lenny to be so friendly with Josh. You know, "Have a soda, Josh," or "Here, try some of this pastry," and "How's the music going? Playing any gigs?"

And every time after he left, Lenny would say, "That's a nice boy." I had a funny feeling Lenny *wanted* me to have a boyfriend, as if he was telling me, "Start growing up, Indian. You can't be my little girl forever." I felt pretty stupid resenting it, and acted awkward and dumb when I was with the two of them. Especially since without Lenny around, I liked Josh. Most girls I suppose would have yelled "Yippee" if their fathers encouraged their boyfriends. But you can know a feeling is silly and still have it.

Lying in bed a couple of weeks after school started, I could hear the rain beating down on the roof. A loose shutter was making a racket. Monday morning, the worst day of the week. I pulled the covers over my head, hoping I would miss the school bus, and that Lenny would let me stay home. But after a while the smell of bacon and coffee drifting up from downstairs was too much. Also Lenny calling, "Hey, Indian, get up."

I did miss the bus, but of course Lenny insisted on driving me to school. On the way we passed a girl in my class, walking with her head down, struggling against the rain and the wind. "Dad, stop, we'll give her a lift."

I introduced Lenny to Anna Weinstein, a tall girl with a pale, thin face and long brown hair, now dripping wet, and fantastic big, brown eyes fringed with heavy lashes. I had never said more than two words to her, and had put her down as someone shy — a brain, and a misfit who kept herself apart as much as I did. Lenny, who knows how to talk to strangers, promptly found out that her father was a doctor, that her family had moved up from New York about five years before because her father wanted a different kind of practice, and that her father liked it here but that she and her mother didn't.

"You and I have that in common," I told her.

She acted surprised. "I don't know why you wouldn't like it. You should have no trouble—your name's not Weinstein."

I kept thinking about what she said and it dawned on me in the middle of my algebra class what she meant: She was Jewish and I wasn't. I was slow on that one. Oh, boy, just what I would expect of the cliques at Compton Falls. Now I really had a good reason to consider them a bunch of creeps. If I needed another reason.

In the afternoon, since we lived in the same direction and we were on the same bus, Anna sat down next to me. "That was nice of your father to stop this morning," she said shyly. "I'm always surprised at how few people do when I miss the bus. I'm always oversleeping."

"I thought in a town like this where everyone knows everyone it would be easy to get a lift."

"I guess they don't know me," she said drily. She had a wide, humorous mouth and a half smile that was nice.

"They don't know me, either, and they probably never will."

"You're a loner, like me. I thought so just watching you in school." Anna's glance made me feel she was glad to find someone like herself.

"I suppose you could call me that. But

we've never stayed in one place long enough for me to make real friends." I told her about how Lenny and I had moved around. "I guess my dad's my best friend," I ended up.

"Do you want to stop off at my house?" She had gathered up her books and was standing up as the bus was pulling up at her corner. I sensed that if I said no, she would never make another move to be friendly. "Sure, thanks."

She lived in a long, low house set back from the street. There was a wing to one side that had a neat sign in front: Reuben Weinstein, M.D. Office. I followed her through a side door that opened into a large, cheerful room with a red tile floor, wood paneling, a big fireplace, and a wall of casement windows. There was a round pine dining table and chairs, and a counter that separated them from the kitchen beyond.

Anna dropped her books on a chair, and called out, "Mom, you home?"

"Yes, I'm here." Anna went through the dining room into a hallway and into a small room off it. I followed her as far as the doorway. Mrs. Weinstein was perched on a high stool in front of a loom, weaving. She didn't stop what she was doing until Anna told her she had brought a friend home. Her mother swung around and greeted me with the same shy smile as Anna's. She was a slim, attractive woman with Anna's deep eyes and pale skin. Anna introduced us and said, "Samantha doesn't like Compton Falls any more than we do."

"I don't mind it. I didn't come up here for any big social life. I mind it for you." There was a worried frown between her eyes.

"Don't worry about me," Anna said.

We went through the hall past a living room and into another wing with bedrooms. "This house goes on and on," I commented. It was a house with unexpected turns, and I liked it.

Anna sat down on her big, four poster bed and motioned me to a chair. She was studying my face.

"What's the matter? I look a mess, don't I?"

"No. I was trying to decide what you were. I think you're a Leo. Are you? When's your birthday?"

"July 22nd."

"I knew it." Her pale face brightened with excitement. "I'm really good at this. I'd sure rather be your friend than your enemy. You hold on to people, don't you? I mean if you really care about someone, you wouldn't be the one to let go. But if you don't like someone, that's it."

"I don't know. I guess I'd hold on to Lenny, my father. He is the only one I've ever really loved. But most daughters love their fathers, don't they?"

"I think with you it's different."

"Sure, because there's just the two of us, and he is different. He's not like other

56

fathers." For some reason the image of Liz Barnes came to my mind. Which had been happening of late: I'd suddenly wonder what she was doing, had she dropped in to see Lenny, had he telephoned her? "Are you serious about astrology?" I didn't feel like talking about Lenny and me.

"I read a lot about it. You'd be surprised how much of it is true. You don't think I'm foolish, do you?" She leaned toward me intently.

"No . . ." I hesitated. I didn't know how much I could level with her. I didn't want to put her down. "I don't know that I believe in it, but I don't know much about it."

"My father thinks it's a lot of hogwash." She sighed. "I wish I could feel about my father the way you do. I get along better with my mom. . . . Oh, well, I guess you can't have everything."

Maybe I was lucky, I thought, not to have to make a choice between two parents. We talked for a while, mostly about school. The fact that she had lived in Compton Falls for five years and still felt that she didn't belong was not very encouraging. Then we went down to the kitchen to have a soda and pretzels. There was something a little sad about Anna, as if she was trying desperately to convince herself that she preferred to be alone, but her heart wasn't in it. There was a music stand in her room and when I asked her what she played, she said the flute. "It's something you can play by yourself. You don't need an accompanist," she said. I thought she sounded somewhat defiant about it, as if she expected an argument.

I was used to being alone — or alone with Lenny, but it wasn't the same way Anna was. For me it was just the way my life happened, but Anna seemed to be making a career of it. You know, "Girl alone against the world" — but I liked her anyway. She had a kind of appeal. I felt there was a lot behind her shyness, and that if she did become a friend, she'd always be a friend. She wasn't a show-off like some of the other girls in school, and I guess our both being loners gave us something in common.

When I said I had to go home, she said she'd walk with me. It was a Monday, so the restaurant was closed, and Lenny was in the kitchen cooking. Again he started chatting with Anna right away. "I'm glad there's a good doctor in town," he said, making conversation. "Every once in a while I get terrible back pains and I need someone to give me a prescription."

"My dad won't just give you a prescription. He doesn't believe in that. He's very thorough; he'll want X-rays to find out why you get backaches. He'll tell you if you want a pain reliever you can get that at the drugstore."

"You mean he'll run up a bill," Lenny said jokingly.

Anna got indignant. "Not at all," she said. "The people around here think he's crazy because he charges so little. And he takes care of plenty of people who don't pay at all."

"I didn't mean anything," Lenny said with his grin. "I don't even know your father. Judging by his daughter he must be a damn fine gent. Here, kids, have some of Ralph's cookies." He opened up a tin and put some on a plate. "By the way, Indian, your boyfriend Josh stopped by. He said you could call him if you want."

Anna looked surprised. "Is Josh Smiley your boyfriend?"

"Of course not." I gave Lenny my dirtiest look. "Don't pay any attention to my father. He doesn't know anything."

"He sure knows how to cook," Anna said, admiring the sauces my father was preparing for the freezer.

After she left I yelled at Lenny. "Why'd you call Josh my boyfriend? Honestly, Dad!"

"You kids are so serious. You can't take anything in fun. But he did say to call him."

"Why should I call him? I'll see him in school."

"That is not exactly the same." Lenny got very busy putting the containers of sauces on racks to cool before putting them in the freezer. I could tell by his face he had something more to say. I had a feeling it was something I wasn't going to like. I was right.

"While Josh was here I said I thought it would be nice if he came over and had dinner with us one night, any Monday, Tuesday, or Wednesday when we're not serving. Maybe you'd like to ask Anna over, too." He was very involved with piling up his dirty pots and dishes in the sink, and his voice was terribly casual.

"What's going on? What do you think you're doing?"

He turned to look at me, with the most innocent, affectionate eyes. "Honey, I thought it was a nice idea."

"Well, you thought wrong. I think I can make my own dates, thank you. When I want you to arrange them, I'll let you know. I assume at least you didn't make a definite date with Josh, did you?"

I eyed him nervously.

"Well, I did say something about Wednesday night. You see," he added hurriedly, "I've asked Liz Barnes to dinner that night and I thought it would be nice if you had a friend, too."

It took a minute to find my voice. I was stunned. "You mean you and I are having a double date?" I asked scathingly.

"Nothing like that, honey. I just thought ...I..." he was sputtering and had the decency to at least look sheepish.

"I can't imagine what you thought. You had better uninvite Josh. I want no part of this. When I want to invite a friend to dinner I think I can manage it myself." He looked so woebegone I almost felt sorry for him. But I was angry. Lenny and I had never had an argument like this before and it bothered me. Suddenly it occurred to me that he was up to something.

"Indian, listen to me, please. I can't un-invite Josh. It would be terrible. Why don't you ask this girl Anna over, too? Then having Josh won't be — well, whatever it is that bothers you. Just asking a boy, I suppose?"

I'd been standing all this time, and now I sat down on a kitchen chair. "What made you ask Liz Barnes to dinner?"

"I thought it was only right. She was very helpful the night we opened. And you were right. She wouldn't take money for the flowers she cut from her own garden. I didn't know how else to thank her, and she is a neighbor. Why? Do you object?"

"I'm not objecting. It's none of my business; you can ask anyone you want." My mind was spinning. *He probably talks to her on the phone all the time. I wonder if she's dropped by for lunch again.*

"I thought she was *your* friend. I thought you liked her?"

"She's alright. Maybe Anna can't come. Then what?"

Lenny laughed. "Then the four of us will have dinner. A good one, too."

"I hope it'll be better than the company."

Anna was able to come, and it was a good dinner. I mean the food. The rest of it was peculiar, at least in the beginning. Mainly because of Lenny. My father is good with people and loves being a host, but that night he was like a nervous bride serving her in-laws for the first time. He burnt some cheese thing he had made as an appetizer, he spilled the wine, and he almost knocked the roast duck off its platter when he was carving it.

Liz thought that was funny, and I knew immediately that although Lenny was embarrassed, her schoolgirl fit of giggles hit him exactly right. He giggled with her and I could practically feel the bond being established between them. They were meeting in some world of their own, and I felt left behind. Suddenly, having to be a hostess for Josh and Anna became a pain, and the unpleasant thought flashed across my busy mind that perhaps Lenny had invited them precisely to keep me occupied. Oh, boy! Here was my father really enjoying himself and I was having suspicious, nasty thoughts like some twerp, pain-in-the-neck, jealous female. Loving someone can get awfully mixed-up. I should have been *glad* my father had found Liz Barnes in Compton Falls; I had been glad when I had met her, and now I was wishing I had walked right past that nursery, or better yet, that it didn't exist.

"Have you planted the bulbs yet?" Liz had turned to me, and I had the distinct feeling she was making a conscious effort to include me in the conversation. "I can help you if you want. I thought they'd be pretty down by the little stream."

"I put them in already." I didn't tell her that was exactly where I'd planted them. She didn't have to try to make me feel at home in my own house. I gave her a sidelong glance. She was wearing a blue necklace the color of her eyes, very little makeup, and I knew, damn it, she was just the kind of woman I would like to be when I grew up. Independent, attractive, not putting on airs, not artificial. She was absolutely different from the other women who had made eyes at Lenny. Fantastically more dangerous.

"That's too bad. It would have been fun to do it together." For a moment I thought with alarm she was going to give me a hug. I imagined the two of us down there digging in the earth, and I knew it would have been fun. But then I watched her turn to Lenny with her open smile, and I could have killed her. It was awful to feel two such different things about a person.

"The only person I ever saw slice a duck like that was a chef in a Chinese restaurant. It's a real art," she said to Lenny.

He grinned. "I'll teach you sometime if you want. It's not that hard." Sucker for flattery.

"I'd love to learn." Suddenly she was all soft and feminine. Ye gods. She had tricks like all the rest, and yet I knew that she wasn't like anyone else. Women. And Dad wanted me to go out with boys and learn how to flutter my eyelashes and tell them how wonderful they were. Well, he'd never get me to do it. Never, never. I'd rather be an old maid and grow warts on my face than look up at some male and pretend he was God's gift from heaven, sent to bring me happiness.

After that, the fantastic food was wasted on me. I kept on being polite to Josh and Anna, but I was conscious every minute of the exchange of glances between Liz and my father, of Liz following him into the kitchen to see how he mixed salad dressing. I was stunned by a strange, new feeling of suddenly becoming Lenny's kid. I had meant it when I'd told Anna that Lenny was my best friend, that I didn't think of us as father and daughter like there was a generation gap between us. We were just Lenny and Indian, and that was all there was to it. But that evening it was as if all of a sudden we changed into ordinary people: Mr. Leonard Thompson, the father, and Miss Samantha Thompson, the daughter; he belonged to the grown-ups, while Samantha the child was relegated to the nursery with the children. It was like a play within a play: I was trying to play my part with Josh and Anna, but all the while I was watching the play taking place between my father and Liz.

Poor Josh. He had been wary about coming in the first place, when I had returned his telephone call. In my dumb way I had started the conversation by saying, "My father said he invited you for dinner on Wednesday. Can you come?"

"What about you? Is it just your father who's inviting me?"

I'm afraid I hesitated a few seconds too long. "Well, no, of course not, but it was his idea."

"You don't sound exactly enthusiastic."

"Don't be silly. Why shouldn't I be?"

"Maybe I have body odor."

I laughed. "You smell as fresh as a baby."

"How would you know? You don't let me get close enough."

"I guess I'm not the cuddly type," I said.

"You can say that again. What time on Wednesday?" he asked.

"That means you'll come, good. Seven o'clock."

"Do I have to wear a tie? I'm not used to dining in fancy restaurants."

"The restaurant's closed on Wednesday. It's just family. Wear anything you want; don't dress up."

Now, I suddenly realized he was saying something to me, and I absently said "Mmm, yes." He looked me straight in the eye and said, "Samantha, you haven't heard a word I said." He followed my eyes over to Liz and Lenny. "She's a neat lady, isn't she?"

"She's okay." Josh didn't say anything, but I thought, *Oh Lord, I hope my crazy thoughts aren't showing*. From that point on I tried to pay attention to my guests.

But after dinner the evening got worse for me. "I hear you're a terrific sax player," Liz said to Josh.

"I play some." He walked over to the upright piano that had come with the house. "Who plays this?"

"Maybe you do," I told him. "I don't."

He looked over some old sheet music that must have been there since the year one. Liz joined him and then she sat down on the bench and ran her hands over the keys. "It's not too bad," she said. "Could stand a tuning. Why don't you get your sax and we could have some music?"

"Great. Come on, Josh, I'll run you home. Do you play anything?" Lenny asked Anna. He was aglow with enthusiasm.

"She plays the flute," I answered for her.

In two minutes the three of them were gone, and I was alone with Liz. "This is nice," she said, "having you and your father as neighbors. I didn't think it would be at first." She laughed. "That shows first impressions shouldn't be taken seriously."

"No, I guess not," I said, still numbed by Lenny's interest in her. Not, I told myself, that I disliked her. She was okay — it was Lenny who had made the turnabout. And that was new, and that was serious. I had always thought I could sense Lenny's moods, know what went on below the surface. But now he had me confused.

The others came back soon, Josh with his

sax and Anna with her flute. Even Anna was different, not so pale, and her eyes were bright and laughing. Liz sat down at the piano, Josh took a position with his sax, and Anna stood to one side so that she could see the music on the piano that Josh had brought. Lenny stood behind Liz with his hand carelessly on her shoulder. The three musicians got their act together, talking for a few minutes, and then Liz struck a note to start.

If ever there was an odd man out, it was me. Lenny pulled me over to him and put his free arm around my shoulder, but his eyes were watching Liz's hands (not grubby) on the keys. We were all singing, mostly off-key, and giggling, and it would have been fun if I hadn't felt an undercurrent of something happening before my own eyes that made me feel separate and alone. It was the weirdest feeling, as though I were a puppet: My face was smiling and I was laughing with the others, and my voice was singing and yet I felt that they were on the inside and I was on the outside, and I was invisible. No one really saw me. There was a paper cutout filling in for me.

I don't know how long we sang around the piano. Then after a while Liz got up, and Josh and Anna played and Liz and Dad did some crazy dancing around the room. I watched. Josh did get me to dance with him a little, but I was terrible. Usually I'm a pretty good dancer, but that night I tripped all over myself like an awkward goat. I don't know what Josh thought.

It was after midnight when Dad said, "Good God, I'd better get you kids home; it's a school night."

Anna threw her arms around me when she said good-bye. "This was the most wonderful evening. I never had such a good time. I'm so glad you and your father moved to Compton Falls." Josh's good-bye to me was on the cool side, but he made a point of thanking my father for having asked him. "A good evening, real neat." And in spite of my preoccupation, I believed him. Liz had walked to our house so she went out with Dad, Anna, and Josh to get a ride home. She gave me a light kiss good-night that took me by surprise and that I could have done without.

"You'd better get to bed, Indian, or I'll never get you up in the morning," Dad said before he left.

I didn't stand at the window and watch them go with tears streaming down my face, but I wasn't so cool, either. It occurred to me that a man is apt to eventually forget a woman he was in love with fifteen years ago, and that a daughter might not be the one chosen to occupy that empty space forever. I went upstairs feeling miserable.

I got undressed, I brushed my teeth and my hair, and I got into bed and listened to my clock ticking. Then I got out and looked out the window. The moon had come up and our grubby lawn looked beautiful with the soft light shining on it. Twelve-thirty. A car came up the road, but it did not turn into our driveway. The house creaked. I got back into bed, and in ten minutes was looking out of the window again. It would take Lenny about five minutes to drop Josh off, then maybe another five for Anna, and then ten minutes to go back to the nursery and leave Liz. Unless he went in with her. *Unless he went in with her.*

Would she offer him a nightcap? Would they talk? Would they kiss? I buried my head in my pillow and cried.

I had known it from the moment we had looked at this house. I had known this was going to happen, I had known it was not going to be peaceful here. I had known I was going to hate Compton Falls. And I realized I was even starting to hate myself. I felt like such a hypocrite: loving my father and having admired Liz, and now resenting their getting together. Feeling those knots in my stomach when I had seen them looking at each other, laughing together, dancing together. A decent daughter would have been happy for her father, and here I was bawling like a spoiled brat. I was ashamed, but I couldn't stop crying.

It was one-thirty when I heard the car in the driveway. I heard Lenny come upstairs; I heard him stop and look into my room to see if I was in bed. I stayed with my face down, on my stomach, hardly breathing until he closed my door softly.

I must have fallen asleep because when I woke up in the morning it took me a few minutes to remember why I felt so tired and depressed.

Chapter Six

"What's for dinner tonight?" I asked Ralph. I was in the kitchen to take my tray up to my room. Lenny had said I could eat in the dining room if I wanted, but I didn't want.

"There's veal scallops, roast lamb, some nice fish, and chicken. There's always chicken." Ralph looked more mournful than usual.

"What's the matter?"

"My father came home from jail."

"Shouldn't that make you happy?"

"You don't know my father. Better when he's in jail. He'll beat up my mother again."

"That's awful, Ralph. Can't you do anything about it? Can't you stop him?"

Ralph almost smiled. "Who, me? What can I do? I tell my mother she should come live with me, but she won't. Maybe she likes it."

"She can't like being beaten." I tried to imagine what his father was like, but I couldn't. I couldn't imagine anyone like that in Compton Falls, it was such a pretty town. Especially in October with the leaves turning into brilliant fall colors. I hadn't seen many New England falls, and every time I went outside I was stunned by the beauty. Yet inside one of the houses, a woman could get beaten up by her husband. It was hard to put together.

"It's hard to imagine that in Compton Falls," I said to Ralph.

He gave his version of a laugh. Kind of a reluctant grunt. "There's plenty that goes on in this town you wouldn't believe," he said darkly.

"I'll take the roast lamb and a lot of potatoes. No squash, but I'll have some salad, and a piece of chocolate cake."

"And a glass of milk," Ralph said.

Up in my room I tried to concentrate on my math, but I was thinking about Josh. I didn't know what to do about him. He'd been kind of following me around, sitting next to me in a special writing class we were in, sitting next to me in gym watching a basketball game.

Today he had asked me to go for a bike ride with him after school. "I thought you had soccer practice?" I said.

"It was called off. Our coach had to be out of town. Neither one of us has to go to the dentist, and you don't have to go home to your father." He was grinning at me, but mocking me, too. A few days ago I had told him I had to go home to my father. It was true, too, because he had promised to take me to a craft show. We went and we had a wonderful time. Lenny bought baskets, and a fantastic hand-knit top for me.

"I'd love to go bike-riding," I said to Josh cheerfully.

"I'll pick you up at your house right after school."

I watched him walk across the school playground. He stopped and played catch for a few minutes with some of the little kids. Everyone liked Josh. He was a good athlete, well-built and strong, someone you would expect to be a fighter. But Josh was easygoing. I had never seen him get angry, although I had a feeling that when he did, he meant it. Everything was up front with him.

On our bike ride I had a taste of his laying everything out. We left the paved road up past the nursery and went on a bumpy but pretty good dirt road. After riding awhile, we stopped to rest in an open field. I stretched out on my back, and Josh sat near me. He was looking down at my face, and I covered my eyes from the sun.

"Don't do that," he said.

"The sun's in my eyes."

"But I like to look at your eyes. I'm trying to figure you out."

"I'm an open book. What's there to figure?"

"Sometimes I think you like me, and other times you're so standoffish."

"Of course I like you. I wouldn't go bike-riding with you if I didn't."

"I don't mean just like. Like you'd like a banana, but if an apple was handy you'd like that as well. I mean really like. You know what I mean."

I turned over onto my stomach. *Oh, God,* I thought, burying my face against the sweet-smelling grass, *he's going to want to kiss me. He's going to want to make love.* For a few wild seconds I thought, *Why not? I'll let him, I'll let him do whatever he wants, he's very attractive, and I'll show Lenny. If he wants to have a love affair with Liz Barnes, I'll have one, too. Why not?*

I turned around and sat up. "I like you, Josh," I said quietly, "but I'm slow. I've moved around so much I've never had a boyfriend, the way you mean a boyfriend, so I'm just not used to the idea." I was trying to be honest, although I knew that wasn't all my reason.

Josh was too smart. "I think there's more to it than that." He looked at me intently. "Your father likes me, doesn't he?"

I was surprised by the question. "Yes, he likes you very much."

"Then it's not that. You're so attached to your father, I thought that if he had something against me, then . . ." He shrugged. "That would keep you away from me."

"It's nothing like that." *You would never understand this in a million years,* I thought, *but my father likes you too much.*

Josh stood up. "Forget it, forget I said anything."

I got up, too. "You're not mad at me, are you?"

"No, of course not." He sounded cool.

I was frightened. With only Anna for a friend, I didn't want to lose Josh. I liked him and I wished he hadn't gotten heavy. "You're not going to drop me, are you?"

Josh swung around. His face was angry, and then he laughed. "Yes, I'm going to drop you on your dumb head. You don't know anything, you don't know anything at all." I honestly didn't know what he meant, so I asked.

Josh stared at me for a few minutes. "You want me to spell it out? You really don't understand?"

I shook my head. He was the one who didn't understand, but that wasn't his fault. How could I tell him that if I wanted a boyfriend he would be it, but that I was afraid to have a boyfriend because I thought my father wanted me to have one. It was all mixed up with the fear of losing Lenny. It sounded pretty crazy to me.

Josh kept looking at me with that "What-am-I-going-to-do-with-her?" expression on his face. "Not everything can be put into words," he said finally. "A guy likes a girl for a lot of reasons. She's attractive, she's bright, she's got something that gets him going. A girl has it for him or she hasn't. You've got it. What more can I say? But a guy doesn't want to make a fool of himself, either. He wants to know if the girl feels the same way. Get it?"

"Yeah." I nodded. I knew he wanted me to say something more. "Please," I said. "Sometime I'll be able to explain it to you." He gave me a helpless look and a shrug, and got on his bike.

We rode home and I thought everything was okay when we said good-bye.

Josh was a burden. Anna says that he has a crush on me, and she says it as if I should be flattered. Just that day, she had looked wistful sitting across from me at lunch. "I think he's mad about you. You've only been in this school a short while, and you've got a boy like Josh falling for you. I've lived here for five years, and the only dates I ever had were with Arthur Kaminsky who stuttered, and he's moved away."

"I know Josh is attractive, but I don't want a boyfriend."

"Are you crazy?" Anna asked seriously.

"I have other things on my mind."

Anna cupped her chin in her hands, stared at me, and then laughed. "I don't dig you. First you complain that everyone's stuck-up, which I agree they are, but then you act stuck-up with someone like Josh, who's nice. Why?"

I fidgeted and moved things around on the table. The salt and pepper, the paper napkins.

Anna wouldn't understand. I had thought of Josh as a friend. But to have him turn into a *boyfriend* was something else. A boyfriend scared me. It was like an intrusion into some private place that belonged to Lenny and me. I wasn't ready for a boyfriend. I had Lenny, something I couldn't explain to Anna. But I still was thinking about it that evening while I stared into space instead of my math book.

The older I got, the more I realized what a special person my father was. When I was little I thought all fathers were like him, but since I was old enough to notice, and I visited kids in their houses, I saw that he was different. I used to believe that even kids who had mothers had fathers who played with them and read to them and took them off on trips, fathers who talked to them. But I'd been learning it's not that way at all. A lot of the girls I met hardly saw their fathers, and when they did they never really talked about anything. I mean talk, not just "When are you going to be home tonight?"

I remember when I was maybe ten, one of the women who worked for us said that I was spoiled for marriage. "You'll never find a man who will cater to you like your father does. He treats you like a little princess — no man's going to fuss over you like that." I had danced around then, making believe I was a little princess, thinking it was a big joke, but now I wondered if she was right.

I did know that other fathers seemed stodgy and old compared to Lenny, always telling their kids what to do but hardly ever doing anything with them. Lenny treated me like an equal, he made me feel intelligent and beautiful. Even though I knew he was prejudiced, it was nice to feel that way. He discussed everything with me.

That very afternoon when I had come home from riding with Josh, he and Ralph were talking about whether Dad should get a liquor license and have a bar.

"That's where the money is, boss," Ralph had said. "You gotta have cocktails."

"I know. I'm only wondering if we shouldn't wait awhile. A license costs a lot, too. Maybe go through the winter as we are."

"But what about the holiday business? Thanksgiving, Christmas, that's when people go out. A lot of folks won't want to travel out to that Harrison House, up the mountain when the weather's bad. They'd come here, but they'd like a couple of drinks before they eat."

I had cut myself a thick slice of Dad's homemade bread, and was eating it and listening. Dad turned to me. "What do you think?"

"I think Ralph's right. A license will cost the same in the spring, but you might have it paid for by then if you got it now."

"You've got a point," Dad had said. "Okay, the vote's two against one, you win. I'll have to borrow some money from the bank, but I'll do it." He grinned at me. "You've got a good head, Indian." Then he added teasingly. "For a girl."

I threw a paper napkin at him.

(As it turned out, the state law was that you couldn't get a liquor license until a restaurant could accommodate a certain number of people and ours wasn't big enough.)

Before I went back to my math, I thought of something else that that woman who had taken care of me had said. I remember her very well, I think she had a crush on Lenny, and she came to call for me at school wearing purple stockings and a raggedy old fur coat. "I suppose someday your father will get married again," she had said, "but I feel sorry for that woman. She'll always be second to you."

Her words hadn't registered at the time, I was too young, but I distinctly remember that the tone of her voice had sent a chill through my gut. I felt that she had put a curse on me.

In school Josh still acted as if he and I were going together, the way he came and sat next to me. I was glad he didn't drop me, although I suspected the subject of our going together was not over between us. The other kids were noticing. A few days later Candy Tuthill and Peggy Roth motioned to me to come and have lunch with them. Anna wasn't in school that day so I didn't have her as an excuse. They were polite and friendly, but when, after a short while, Candy asked me if I was dating Josh, I knew they were on a fishing trip.

"No, I'm not dating anyone," I said.

That surprised them. "We were sure you were." Peggy had a cute, round face and a dumpy figure. "We thought if you were you'd come to our Halloween party with him." She looked at Candy questioningly, as if she didn't know how to say what she wanted to.

But I'm not dumb, and I caught on. I smiled brightly. "Well, I'm really not. And I'm sure you don't want an extra girl at your party. It's all couples, isn't it?"

Peggy nodded. But Candy spoke up. "Would you come if we asked Josh to bring you?"

"I'd feel funny." I didn't want them, or anyone, arranging dates for me. "Let's skip it. I may have to stay home and help out in my father's restaurant," I lied glibly. "Halloween will probably be a big night, holidays usually are. But thanks anyway."

But Candy didn't drop it. She was a striking looking girl, with long blonde hair, a good figure, and good clothes that showed it off. Besides which, she got very good marks. "I think Josh is very attractive, don't you?"

"He's okay. Why don't you just invite him, anyway?"

Both girls giggled, and I sensed in a flash that Candy very much wanted Josh to come to their party, and for some reason had decided that asking me was the way to get him there. That struck me as funny. Josh certainly wasn't playing hard to get with me. But if there was one thing I hated it was the dopey intrigue about boys that so many girls went in for, and I was going to stay out of it.

"Maybe I will," Candy had said, and she gave me a smile that seemed to say I might be sorry. Well up yours, I thought to myself — a vulgar expression but it fit my feelings perfectly. If she thought I was about to compete with her for Josh's attention, she was greatly mistaken.

"I'm sure he'd love to come, alone or with some other girl," I said amiably.

"Is he dating someone?" Candy asked sharply.

"I haven't the faintest idea."

"I haven't seen him with anyone," Peggy murmured.

I finished my lunch and got up. "It was nice having lunch with you. Enjoy your party." I walked away from them feeling I had just navigated an obstacle race and come out the winner. But I wasn't playing hard to get; I just didn't want to play.

However, that afternoon Josh was waiting for me after school. "It's a nice day," he said. "Let's walk home instead of taking the bus. I'll buy you a soda."

"Wow. The last of the big spenders." I saw Candy and Peggy standing on the school steps watching us go off together. I couldn't help but giggle.

"What's funny?" Josh looked at me and then followed my eyes. "Oh them. Are you going to their Halloween party?"

"No. Are you?"

"I was going to ask you to go with me. Will you?"

"Were you invited?" I was really getting curious.

"Yes, and I said I'd come if I could bring my own date. That meant you."

Things were becoming clear. "I don't like parties very much, especially with a lot of people I don't know."

"That's the way you'll get to know them. Don't you want to make friends here?" Josh was steering me toward an ice-cream store.

"Not especially." I looked at Josh and realized how awful I sounded.

"I'm beginning to think you really are a snob." Josh led me inside and we sat down at a booth.

"I'm not, I'm really not. I told you, it takes me a long time to make friends, and I've never had that kind of time. We've moved so much, Lenny and me. I've had a different kind of life from most kids. I guess I'm conditioned to being alone, or with my father."

"You really worship your father, don't you?" Josh made it sound like that was peculiar.

"We get along well. What's wrong with that?"

"Nothing. Except no boy's going to measure up to him in your eyes."

"Well, maybe not." I laughed. "So I'll be

an old maid and live with my father. I can think of worse things."

Josh flashed his bright, intelligent eyes at me. "Your father," he said, "may have other ideas. Do you want a soda or a sundae?"

We both got chocolate sundaes with sprinkles and didn't talk any more about the Halloween party. But when we walked home, Josh said that the following Monday we only had school for half a day because of a teachers' conference. "You want to go to Island Park with me?"

"What's Island Park?"

"An amusement park. It's terrific, it's got rides that will knock your teeth out. I think I can get Mom's car."

"I don't know as I want my teeth knocked out. . . . I'll have to ask my father."

Josh gave me a disgusted look. "You're hedging. Don't come back and tell me you have to peel potatoes for the restaurant, or some cock-and-bull story like that. If you don't want to go, say so."

Lenny had said he wanted to explore the area one afternoon on a day the restaurant was closed, and I thought that would be a good time to do it. I didn't want to make a firm date with Josh. "I'm not hedging, but I'll have to let you know. Call me tonight if you want."

"Okay. But say yes. You'll have fun, I promise you."

I went down to the kitchen later in the eve-

ning, after the dining room was thinning
out. Ralph and Lena and Mary were all excited about a murder that had happened in
a nearby town. "That woman's son didn't
do it. They got no right holding him. It's
not fair." Lena was real exercised about it.

"You don't know." Ralph was mournfully
examining a basket of tomatoes, picking out
those too rotten to use. "Some sons want to
kill their fathers. This one was a stepfather."
He sounded ominous.

Lena glanced at him. "Don't talk that way.
You give me the shivers. I know that boy.
He wouldn't kill anyone. He's a nice boy."

"They always say that," Mary said, wiping
the silver ferociously. "I read once about a
boy went to Sunday school every week, said
his prayers at night, and one day he killed
everyone in his family. Just like that. The
neighbors all said he was so nice. You never
know."

I perched at the edge of a table and listened. Grown-up conversation was much
more interesting than kids'. They talk about
real life.

"What you doing down here?" Lenny came
into the kitchen.

"I have to ask you something. We have a
half-day holiday on Monday — teachers' conference. Josh asked me to go to an amusement park, but I don't want to go if you can
go exploring. Remember, you said you wanted
to when there was a free afternoon."

"This Monday? I don't know, there are a

lot of things I have to do around here. You go along with Josh; we can go anytime."

"You sure?"

"Sure, I'm sure. Go ahead, you'll have a good time."

Everyone wanted me to have a good time. But to me it sounded like they were saying "Go to the dentist, you'll enjoy it."

Chapter Seven

Lenny was in the kitchen when I came down on Monday morning. "You'll have a good day," he said after kissing me good morning. "The weather report was cool, sunny, a perfect fall day."

"Would have been a good day to go exploring." I poured myself a glass of orange juice.

"This'll be more fun. By the way, I may be home late." I was beginning to recognize that ultra casual note in his voice that meant he was going to say something I wouldn't like. "Why don't you and Josh eat out? Here's some money." He handed me twenty dollars. "You can keep the change," he said with a grin. Now I knew I wasn't going to like what was coming.

"I thought you had to do things around the house. Where are you going?" I could sound as casual as he.

"Liz is taking me over to some herb farm. She thinks we should have an herb garden.

It's a great idea, don't you think? Fresh herbs from our own garden?"

'Terrific. And I suppose she offered to take care of it, too." My sarcasm went past him. I didn't look at him while I broke up my shredded wheat into a dish. "I thought you didn't want to be bothered with the outdoors yet."

"We'll probably plant the garden in early spring. But she thought it would be a good idea to go over and see what they have and order what I want. Besides, she said it was a beautiful ride. I invited her out to dinner. That's the least I can do. So don't worry if I get home late."

"Why should I worry?" Lenny turned around then and looked me full in the face. My stupid mug as usual gave me completely away, and Lenny could tell how angry and hurt I was.

"What's the matter, Indian? What's bothering you? You don't like Liz?" There was an anxious note in his voice.

I wasn't going to answer that question. "You told me you had things to do around here. I wouldn't have made the date with Josh if you said you wanted to go out."

"This isn't what I'd call going out. It's a business trip, for the restaurant." He grinned at me, knowing as well as I how silly he sounded.

"I don't really care. But next time you want to make a date to go out, you don't have to lie to me."

"Come on, baby, that's not fair. I didn't lie. This came up later, after you told Josh you were going with him. I thought it worked out fine — you'd be out and I'd be out."

"Forget it, it really doesn't matter." I was dying to know whether the idea had been his or Liz's, but I wasn't going to ask. After all, I thought mournfully, what difference did that make?

The afternoon with Josh started out okay. Josh decided we shouldn't eat lunch at school, so we picked up huge salami-and-cheese sandwiches at a deli, and sodas, and ate at a picnic table at Island Park. "Sure beats the junk they give you in school," Josh said. "I don't know how you eat that stuff after eating in your father's restaurant. Must be fun living in a restaurant. Your father's real neat, too. I like him."

"Don't you like your parents?"

"They're okay. Of course I like them, but we're not friends the way you are with your dad. We don't do many things together. My parents play golf, an old people's game. On a vacation once I got them to go bike-riding with me, but they complained it was too much like work. Then I tried to interest my dad in tennis, but that didn't work either. I'm not putting them down, they're really great, but I think they believe in a generation gap. They think parents should be parents, not pals. My mom's a lot into psychology and she believes I should do my thing and they should do theirs. I don't think she'd approve of your being so buddy-buddy with your father."

"You think I'm too chummy with him? But that's the way it is. We're very close. I guess because there's just the two of us."

"Someday there may be three of you," Josh said, taking a big bite of his sandwich. "I think he's sweet on Liz Barnes, the lady who has the nursery."

"What makes you say that?" I asked sharply.

"A couple of afternoons when you stayed late in school — remember, you wanted to use the library for a book report — I saw them out walking. I was riding my bike. They were holding hands."

"So what? People walk that way all the time. To keep from falling. My father doesn't get sweet on people. That's a ridiculous thing to say."

"You don't have to bite my head off," Josh said huffily. "I just said I *thought* he was, and you can make what you want of it. I don't know what you're so excited about."

"I'm not excited."

After lunch the afternoon went downhill all the way. It was like the story of the king chopping off the head of the messenger who had brought bad news. I was furious with Josh for saying what he did about Lenny and Liz. So every time I started to have a good time on one of the rides, I'd look at Josh and remember what he had said and I'd think of

Lenny and Liz riding in her convertible out to the herb farm, and I'd feel sick and take it out on Josh. On the Whip, and in the Plane Ride, and on the Ferris wheel, Josh would put his arm around me, and I'd wriggle away.

Finally, on the Thunderbolt, the steepest roller coaster I'd ever seen, I sat away from Josh as far as I could. I was scared stiff, but I didn't want to be so close. "What's the matter with you?" he asked.

"Nothing." I sounded sullen, and he shut up.

The thing started, and I clutched the rail hard. But it was awful. I thought my head was going to snap off, the way we went up and then zoomed down, and I was sure my stomach was going to fall out. "Hang on," Josh said, and he grabbed hold of me again. Like a fool I pulled away again, and he got mad, and sat away from me as far as he could get. When at last we got off, his face was grim and I was sick to my stomach but determined not to let him know.

"Let's go home," Josh said.

"Don't you want to go out to eat?" I asked weakly, food being the last thing in the world I wanted.

"Not particularly," he said. He walked toward the parking lot, and I followed. *Oh, Lord,* I thought, *if I have to get into a car now I'll surely throw up.*

"You angry at me?" I asked, trying to sound innocent.

"You're not very friendly."

"I'm sorry if you didn't have a good time."

"So am I." Then he stopped and looked at me. "If you didn't like me you shouldn't have come out with me. I don't like being pushed away."

"Well, I don't like being mauled over," I said, just as coldly as he.

Josh laughed. "Mauled over?" He kept on laughing, uproariously. "You are about the dumbest girl I ever knew. I had you all wrong in the beginning. I thought you were pretty neat, but I sure made a mistake. Come on, I'll take you home to Daddy, who can protect you from big, bad boys like me."

He got into the car and slammed his door behind him. I got into my side and curled up as close to the door as I could get. "You can sit in back if you want to," Josh said. "Maybe you'll feel safer back there."

"Shut up," I said crossly.

Josh started the car with a jerk, and he had just about pulled out of the parking lot, when I knew I couldn't make it. "Stop the car," I yelled. "I've got to get out." Josh slammed on the brakes and pulled up at the side of the road. I ran out and threw up in some bushes. At least Josh had the decency not to come out and watch.

When I got back into the car he said, "Feeling better?"

"I suppose so."

We rode back to Compton Falls in silence. Not a nice, friendly silence, but an awful one. When the car swerved around a corner I had to hang on so as not to fall against him. We were terribly careful not to touch each other. When we were getting near to my house I was feeling guilty, still sick to my stomach, and miserable. I dreaded staying home alone the whole evening waiting for Lenny to come home. "You sure you don't want to go out to eat?" I asked.

"Do you?"

"I'm not really hungry, but . . ."

"Then what's the sense of going out?" Josh reached over and opened the door on my side. "See you around."

"Thanks for all the rides," I said lamely and got out of the car.

The house was quiet and empty. It was worse than just an ordinary empty house because usually it was so busy and filled with people, the staff and the guests. I ran up to my room and flung myself on my bed. It was a beautiful dusk. The sky was all rose-tinted from the setting sun, and I could tell it was going to be a gorgeous evening. A romantic evening for Lenny and Liz. I lay on my back and tried to imagine what it was like to fall in love. Did they want to kiss all the time? What did they talk about? Would they go to bed together? Every time I pictured Lenny taking Liz in his arms, my stomach, which was still pretty unsteady, turned over. I rolled over and buried my face in my pillow. What would happen to me if Lenny married Liz?

I had no one but Lenny. As far as I was

concerned, his father in South America could be living on the moon. His Christmas cards could be coming from a stranger.

I could run away, but where would I run to? Besides, I didn't want to run away. I wanted to stay with Lenny all my life, and with no one else.

The house creaked, and once the telephone rang and I ran like crazy to answer it, but whoever it was had hung up. The house kept making funny noises. Eventually I guess I fell asleep. When I woke up it was pitch black. I sat up on the bed, still in all my clothes. I heard a door open downstairs, and I flew out into the hall.

"Lenny, Lenny, is that you?"

"Darling, what's the matter?" Lenny switched on the light. "What are you doing up and dressed? It's very late."

"I fell asleep with my clothes on." I ran down the stairs and hugged him hard. "I'm so glad you're home. I'm so glad."

Lenny held me for a minute and then gently pushed me away to look at me. "Are you all right? Did you have a good time?"

"So-so. Did you?"

"Yes, Indian; yes, I did. A very good time." His face had something in it, a kind of tenderness that came over it like when he spoke about my mother or when he was showing a special feeling for me.

"Lenny, are you in love with Liz Barnes?"

Lenny grinned. "Honey, it's so late." He lifted my face and touched my cheek reassuringly. "Let's not talk about it now, Indian. Go on up to bed."

"You are, I know you are."

"We'll talk about it some other time, not in the middle of the night."

I walked back upstairs slowly, my heart touching bottom. He had given me a hug when he came in, but he hadn't kissed me good-night. He hadn't asked me to come into the kitchen and tell him about my day. I could hear him downstairs puttering around. He wanted to be alone to think about Liz. He wasn't going to think about me anymore. I was no longer "Miss First" with him, as he sometimes said. I wanted to die.

I got nowhere with Lenny when I asked him again the next day if he was in love with Liz. He laughed it off and told me he wasn't sure what being in love meant. But I knew he was. I could tell after that day by the way he ran for the phone when it rang, and I always knew when she was the one who was calling. I could tell by the way he lowered his voice, spoke into the phone as if he was whispering softly into someone's ear, and by his face when he asked her to hang on so he could take the call up in his room. I think they talked to each other a couple of times a day, and I'm sure they saw each other when I was at school. Lenny didn't have much time to go out at night, but on the nights the restaurant was closed, he began to go out for a little while after our supper. I didn't ask him where he was going, and he didn't tell me.

There was a wall between us that neither one of us wanted to jump.

About a week or so later, Anna and I were having lunch. "So what, so I flunked a math exam," I said to her scolding. "What's so terrible about that? Who cares about math anyway?"

"I thought you did. Also, you didn't do your book report. Mr. Worden was really pissed off." Anna was looking at me like I was breaking out in a rash. "What's the matter with you? Something's eating you, Sammy."

"Nothing's eating me, and Mr. Worden can go fly a kite."

"I thought you liked him. Something is the matter with you, but if you don't want to talk about it, okay. But you're not fooling me."

"Do I look that bad?" I knew Anna was being sympathetic. She was not the kind to pry.

"You don't look great. I've seen you look better. If it's Josh, and whatever happened between you — and I'm not asking you what it was — for what it's worth I think he'd like to make up. He's going around looking pretty mopey, too. He asked me if you were still mad at him. I told him I didn't know. Are you?"

"Josh? No, I'm not mopey about Josh. I'm not mad at him, either. It has nothing to do with Josh. When I was annoyed with him it really wasn't his fault in the first place."

"You ought to tell him that. Put him out of his misery."

"He can't be miserable because of me. That's ridiculous."

"But I think he is." Anna said it like some indisputable fact.

Her statement made me feel uncomfortable. I didn't want Josh to be miserable about me, the thought felt like a heavy weight. Thinking about Josh was too much then: My feelings were so mixed, I didn't want to have to deal with them. Just thinking about anyone being in love with me made me feel sick. I didn't want to talk about it. "I'll be okay," I said to Anna.

I suppose it was inevitable that Mr. Worden would say he wanted to have a talk with me. My marks were getting worse, and I knew my attitude was lousy. The worst part was that I didn't care. I was already figuring on not living in Compton Falls for very long. If Lenny did marry Liz, I wasn't going to hang around. I couln't bear to watch someone take over Lenny. I could see signs of it already. I used to beg Lenny to stop smoking, and he'd cut down for a while and then start up again. Now he had stopped. Really quit, cold turkey. "You can thank your friend Liz," he said with a grin. "She showed me what nicotine does, and besides, it makes her sick."

"Good for her," I said unenthusiastically, although I was glad he'd quit. But why for her and not me?

It was on a Friday that I stayed after school to meet with Mr. Worden. His pink, round face was serious, and I expected a bawling out. But that wasn't his style. "I'm worried about your marks," he started off, "and I'm worried about you. You started out such a good student, but something has happened. I wish I knew what." He looked at me expectantly. "Are you having trouble making friends in a new place? I wish you'd tell me what's bothering you."

There's something weird about me, because when I feel awful and anyone is especially kind to me, I burst into tears. I didn't want to bawl in front of Mr. Worden, so I mumbled that I was okay, and I was sorry my marks had gone down. He gave me a bit of a pep talk and said he knew how hard it was to come to a new school and a new town but since he had the impression I'd been on my own so much he hadn't expected me to have a lot of trouble. I told him I'd work harder and that was that.

I had to walk home since I'd missed my bus, and when I got to our house, I kept walking. I suddenly decided to go up past the nursery. I'd been thinking about it before, kind of like someone wanting to go back to the scene of the crime, wanting to see Liz and half afraid to.

Even though the weather had turned cold and gray, she was working outdoors. I had thought I'd walk by unnoticed, but she saw me and called to me to come in. I guess I had some vague hope that if I did see her I'd find she'd turned ugly or was different. But she wasn't. She looked marvelous in a blue work shirt and jeans, healthy and glowing. She acted the same as always, natural and friendly, just as if nothing had happened. For a few minutes I hated her for behaving that way. How dare she be so two-faced, pretending she was my friend when she was ruining my life?

But she was fantastic, so open, I forgot that I wanted to hate her. "Isn't it great that your father stopped smoking? Is he frightfully irritable at home? I meant to call you to warn you that he probably would be. You really deserve the credit, you know. He said you'd been after him for ages, and then I guess I was the straw that broke the camel's back. It doesn't matter, really, the important thing is he's done it, and I think it will stick, don't you?"

"I hope so. What are you doing?" She was taking plants out of the ground.

"Getting ready for winter. I'm going to pot these and keep them in the greenhouse. They're houseplants and can't take the winter outside. Do you want any? I have lots of babies here. Would you like some impatiens — there are some marvelous colors?"

"I haven't any money."

"I offered them to you, Samantha. I wasn't trying to sell them."

"My father said that since this was your

business, we should pay for whatever we take."

She laughed merrily. "Did he say that? Then I guess I'd better pay him every time I have lunch with him at the restaurant. Pick out what you want, the colors are marked on the pots."

"Do you have lunch with him often?" The question was out before I could stop myself.

She gave me a sharp look. "Pretty often, I guess." She hesitated as if she wanted to be careful about what she said. "Your father and I have become good friends." Then she looked up at me, with that direct look she had Her eyes were very blue. "Does that bother you?"

"Why should it?"

"It shouldn't, but that doesn't mean it doesn't. I'd like us to be friends, too." She spoke softly.

"Because you're my father's friend doesn't mean you have to be mine. He has friends and I have friends. He's had friends before," I said meanly.

She laughed again. "I'm sure he has, lots of friends. Men and women. You're very devoted to your father, aren't you?"

"Like most daughters." I was hardening myself against her.

She shook her head. "No, I don't think that's quite true. I think you are more dependent on your father than most daughters. That's understandable under the circumstances."

"But that's not true," I said angrily. "I'm very independent. My father will tell you that."

"Your father adores you," she said soothingly. "I meant dependent in a different way — emotionally. You are independent for a girl your age. You know how to be alone and how to take care of yourself. But your life revolves around your father, and that's a dependency most daughters don't have."

"You make it sound as if it's something wrong. Yes, my father is the most important person in my life, the only important one. He always has been and he always will be. Nothing is ever going to change that." I stared at her defiantly, glad that I had spoken up. Everything was out in the open now. I didn't care how blue her eyes were or how nice she was, I was glad that she knew she couldn't take my father away so easily. She'd be up against me.

She got the picture. She just kept looking at me coolly with a little smile. "You might be right, Samantha, maybe nothing ever will change that. I would feel very sorry though if you never found a man of your own who would become more important to you." Then she smiled at me brightly. "If you pick out the plants you want, I'll drop them off at your house later."

"I don't want any plants, thank you. It'd be a bother remembering to water them, and you wouldn't want them to die."

"No, I wouldn't." She still had that little

smile on her face as she watched me get up from the ground where I'd been squatting. I said good-bye and left.

I walked home slowly, wondering if I had come out of that as well as I thought I had. I wasn't sorry I had said what I did, but I had a funny feeling that she had been partly feeling sorry for me and partly laughing at me. I didn't like it either way. *And*, I thought with a sinking heart, *what is she going to go back and tell my father?*

Chapter Eight

Nothing changed after my meeting with
Liz. Except perhaps that she and my father
were more open about seeing each other. She
was at the restaurant a lot in the evenings,
and almost always had dinner with Lenny
on the nights the dining room was closed.
Instead of staying downstairs with them I
took a tray up to my room, saying I had
homework to do, the same as I did the nights
Lenny was busy working.

After a few weeks of that routine, one
afternoon when I came home from school
my father said he wanted to talk to me. I
knew darn well what he wanted to talk about.

"There's nothing much to talk about," I
said to him. We were in the kitchen. He was
filling shells with meat, and I fixed myself
a sandwich.

"There's a lot to talk about. Wait till I get
these in the oven and we can sit down and
talk."

"I have homework to do."

"You can do it later. You're not going to slide out of this, Indian, and don't give me that innocent look. You're not fooling me, I know you too well."

"You don't know how I look, you have your back to me." I watched him put his meat pies into the oven.

"I know without looking at you."

We sat facing each other across a small table. Lenny had a cup of coffee. "Why are you avoiding Liz Barnes whenever she comes over here? I think it's quite rude of you to eat up in your room when she's here."

I thought about that for a few minutes. "Maybe I don't like her."

Lenny's dark eyes narrowed. "I don't believe that. You liked her very much. If I really thought you didn't like her, things would be different."

"How different?" I was watching his face. He's like me, everything shows, and now he wanted to choose his words carefully.

"Let's not beat around the bush, Sammy." He stopped cracking his knuckles, a habit he has when he's tense, and he relaxed slowly against the back of his chair. "I don't think I would ever be attracted to a woman you didn't like. Our tastes are too much the same. It just wouldn't happen."

"You're in love with her, aren't you?"

We held each other's eyes for minutes. "I think so," he said. "It's all very new. We're both feeling our way. She's an extraordinary woman, and she doesn't make a commitment easily. But if and when she does, it would be all out. I think she's afraid of you."

I almost smiled. It had been what I wanted, for her to be afraid of me, to go away because of me. But now, looking at Lenny's face when he talked about her, I felt I was the one who should disappear. He really loved her, and that broke my heart.

"She doesn't have to be afraid of me," I said. "If you and she love each other, that's fine. When are you going to get married?"

"Don't put on an act with me, Indian. I know better. You're not behaving like a happy kid who wants her father to get married. Why don't you level with me? Tell me what's eating you?"

"Flies," I said flippantly, suddenly swatting one. "Am I supposed to set off fireworks because you want to get married? You're a grown-up, you don't need my approval. And you can tell Liz Barnes I won't be in her way, I'll go to boarding school. She can have you all to herself." I stood up to go upstairs, but Lenny came over to me. For the first time in my life I didn't want him to touch me, I didn't want his arms around me. I couldn't bear it if he was going to kiss me. Our life together was over, everything was over. I wanted to be miles and miles away, and I wanted to be alone.

Some instinct must have told him how I felt, or maybe it was in my face. He didn't touch me, he just faced me with an expression of such misery and tenderness I almost gave in to throwing my arms around him. But I didn't.

"Liz doesn't want me all to herself," he said simply. "If we ever do get married, we want the three of us to be a family. It's not an either/or proposition, Sammy, and don't make it one."

"Maybe it is for me," I said, looking away from him.

I ran up to my room, feeling ashamed, angry, hurt, miserable. I didn't have to wonder about it anymore, now I knew. And I meant it when I said I'd go to boarding school. I would never, never live in this house with my father and his wife. With a stepmother. The very word made me feel sick, and the crazy thing was, my feelings had so little to do with Liz. If Lenny wasn't in love with her, I knew I would like her. He was right when he said he probably wouldn't be attracted to someone I didn't like, one of those artificial ladies who flirted with him. Liz was different, and it made it even worse because I could see why he would fall in love with her. He wouldn't need anyone else when he had her. I had had glimpses of it already, when I'd seen the two of them together. They could shut out the world.

They could be *happy* together. The thought set off a flood of tears I couldn't stop. I felt so terribly ashamed. I must be a monster: I, who loved Lenny so much, who thought my love was so special, was miserable because he had found someone who could make him

happy in a way I never could. I should slit
my wrists and watch the blood ooze out and
all my bad feelings with it. I wept for the
meanness in me and the loneliness, and somewhere deep down I felt a knot of anger.
Lenny should never have let me love him so
much, he should have known that someday
he would leave me. I wept with deep, terrible
sobs as if somehow I had to suffer pain to
pay for all the good times Lenny and I had
had together. And to pay for my own selfish-
ness. What a jerk I was to have thought that
Lenny and I would always be together in our
own sunny garden — that's how I thought
of us, two people who had lived in a special
place that had no storms or clouds. I cried
until I was exhausted, and when I got up and
looked at myself in the mirror I couldn't believe I still looked the same, except for my
red eyes. I felt a million years old. I felt like
I could never be optimistic again, never again
think that the world was pretty. A whole
part of me, the fun part, seemed to have disappeared, forever.

After our conversation in the kitchen,
Lenny acted as if he had never told me he
was in love and might marry Liz. I don't
understand how people can have great emo-
tional encounters and then act like nothing
happened. Grown-ups do that all the time;
they yell at each other, or cry, and the next
minute they're talking to each other as if
they were best friends. I never thought be-

fore that Lenny was like that. But now he was. If it wasn't that Liz was still around, and they looked at each other like two dopey kids, grinning at each other foolishly, I might have thought I'd made it all up. Hadn't he heard what I'd said? Didn't he know I was going to leave if he got married? Didn't he care?

I tore out clippings from magazines advertising boarding schools and left them lying around, but Lenny paid no attention. I made myself scarce whenever Liz came over, but Lenny didn't say anything more to me about taking my tray upstairs. Liz was cordial, even friendly, asking me about school and stuff, but she kept her distance, too. I had the feeling of an ominous lull before a big storm. Like two armies getting into position for a major battle.

Before Christmas vacation Anna told me that Josh wanted to ask me to a dance. "He does?" I responded with mixed feelings. We were at her house on a Saturday afternoon. She had some new records we were listening to.

"He thinks you'll think he's running after you. Putting on the pressure." Anna was on the floor and she leaned over to turn the record.

"But that's silly. I like Josh. I just didn't get excited about his being my boyfriend. You know, more than just a friend. Maybe he came on too fast for me. I'm slow." I looked at her with a weak smile.

"Like heck you are. I don't understand you."

"That's what Josh said. We had a fight at the amusement park. I was feeling lousy that day and I think he's being oversensitive. I overreacted, and anyway, I thought we had sorted it out."

"You haven't been very nice to him."

I got up and changed a record. "I suppose I haven't." I turned to face Anna. "I haven't been nice to my father, either. I'm a mess. Tell Josh that if he wants to ask me to a dance, he doesn't have to go through you."

"Maybe he's shy."

"I think *you* like him. Why don't you go with him?"

"Because he likes you, that's why."

The following Monday, Josh and I met in the hall. Suddenly we were face to face. "Hello." He stopped me.

"Hello." He looked terribly attractive.

"How're you doing?"

"Okay. You?"

"Fine." I knew he wanted to say something more, and I realized how shy he was. All of a sudden I wanted to touch him, to put my hand on his cheek. I didn't want him to look at me so warily. "Anna gave me a message from you," I said.

His face brightened, and he grinned. "Good old Anna. Will you come with me? It's a dance at the High next Saturday night."

"Sure. What time?"

"I'll let you know." His grin widened. "It's the big dance of the year. Christmas dance. Everyone gets dressed up."

I grinned, too. "I think I can manage."

He gave me a swift look, to make sure I wasn't being sarcastic. "You'll be the belle of the ball."

Saturday morning everything was hectic. There were a lot of reservations for dinner that night, and one special, big private party that Lenny was excited but a little nervous about. The police commissioner and his wife were giving a dinner party. He was a bigwig in the area and Lenny wanted everything to be super. Apparently Commissioner Larkin could bring us a lot of business.

I was having a fit because the hot water ran out when I wanted to wash my hair. "Oh," Lenny said absently, "it'll be plenty hot by tonight when we need it."

"I'm not worried about tonight. I need it now."

"You'll just have to wait until it gets hot again." Lenny never used to talk to me that way. "Liz said she was bringing some flowers over from the greenhouse. I wonder where she is." He kept looking out the window.

"Maybe she fell in the pond." If I had wanted his attention, I got it.

"What kind of a thing is that to say? It's not funny, Samantha." Lenny spun around furiously. I couldn't remember when he had last called me Samantha.

"Maybe you've losing your sense of humor."

"Maybe you're getting too fresh." He was talking to me like any ordinary father, not like Lenny. He wasn't even looking like Lenny. He looked stern and had a "don't you fool around with me" expression on his face. It was worse than a slap.

"Yes, sir." I said and marched back upstairs to my room. He didn't follow me. I waited in my room hoping he would come in, as he always did whenever there was a fuss between us. But he didn't. I looked out of my window when I heard a car drive up, and watched Liz get out. Lenny ran out to meet her. They kissed and Liz said something that made him laugh, and together they brought the flowers into the house. He didn't care about me, or my hot water, or whether I lived or died. For a while I hated both of them.

Sometime in the afternoon the crisis erupted, if a crisis can erupt. Lena, who had been sniffling all week, called up to say she had come down with a fever and probably the flu, and couldn't come to work. Lenny got into a rage, unlike him, and yelled, "Why the devil didn't she stay home and take care of herself instead of waiting till today to get sick?"

Ralph, in his doleful way, said, "She could still be sick today."

"What are we going to do?" I'd never seen Lenny so upset.

"I can wait on tables. I'll stay home." I was excited by the idea. I had been nervous about the dance, anyway — who would dance with me besides Josh? And being there to work with Lenny might bring us back to old times. Maybe he'd remember how much fun we always had, even when we'd been broke or he was in between jobs, and he'd forget about Liz. "I'd love to do it."

Lenny looked at me but he wasn't really seeing me. His mind was elsewhere. "I'll call up Liz, I bet she'd come in and help." He grinned, delighted with himself. "She'll think it's a real lark." He was on his way to the telephone.

"You didn't here what I said," I yelled. "I said I could do it. Please, Lenny, let me."

He turned around. "Don't be silly, Indian. You have a date to go to a dance, and besides, you're a little young to be a waitress. Hadn't you better get along and use that hot water you've been waiting for?"

I went upstairs to my room. I didn't cry, I didn't even feel angry. I don't know what I felt, except terribly sad. I took out the one picture of my mother and sat and looked at it. "I wonder if he's forgotten all about you, too," I said softly. I took the picture over to the window. She looked so bright and full of fun, and pretty. Prettier than Liz. Why did she have to go and die?

Then I cried. I would look awful that night with red eyes and swollen eyelids, but I didn't care. I cried the way I had that night a short while ago, deep sobs that almost choked me. And I felt the same kind of shame. I was a rotten kid. When I stopped I could hear the kitchen noises from downstairs, and Lenny going back and forth to the dining room, whistling. *Okay*, I thought. *You've got your life. I'll have mine. I'll do something, I'm not sure what, but it's not going to be around here. If it won't be boarding school, it will be something else. You probably won't even care.*

I kept washing my face in cold water to get rid of the puffiness, but I thought I still looked pretty lumpy. I brushed my hair hard and put on mascara, and doused myself with the perfume our last landlady had given me. I wore a thin chiffon India-print dress with terrific dark plum and pale colors. I didn't look half bad. When I went downstairs people were already coming into the dining room and when I saw Liz wearing an apron (Lena's uniform would never fit her; Lena was fatter), I almost laughed.

Liz came over to me in the hall. "You look lovely, just beautiful." She stood back and studied me. "You have a beautiful throat and shoulders, but with that scoop neck something around your throat would look nice. Would you like to borrow this?" She put her hand to a delicate gold chain she was wearing. It had a tiny garnet and pearl charm on it. "It's antique and I think it would go perfectly with your dress." She wore it a lot of the time, and I had secretly admired it.

"No, no, thank you. I'd rather not."

"Are you sure? Why don't you try it on?"

We looked at each other steadily for a minute. "No, thanks anyway. I'm sure."

She hesitated a moment. "I'd like to be friends with you, Samantha."

I just stood facing her and then turned away. "I'd better go say good-bye to Lenny. Josh'll be here any minute." I went into the kitchen.

"Have a good time," she called after me. "A really good time."

Even Ralph grumpily said I looked good, and Jerry let out a low whistle. "You look so grown-up," Lenny said, as if he hadn't seen me for years. "You look gorgeous. Did Liz see you?"

He made me feel like Exhibit A. "I saw her in the hall. Good-night. Hope your dinner party's terrific."

"And you have a good time." Lenny kissed me. "It's nice having a gorgeous daughter," he said and hugged me. Josh was in the hall, so I got my coat and left.

A dance was the last thing in the world I felt like, but I really didn't want to spoil Josh's fun for the second time. Also I didn't want to think about my father and Liz. I made up a story to amuse Josh and me. "Once, when Lenny was broke and didn't have the money to pay for a motel room we were in, I went to the police station and cried and said I needed fifty dollars to get to my grandmother's. But they couldn't call her because she'd be too worried about me. But I said I'd leave my watch, a good one, and when I sent them the fifty they could send me back the watch."

"Did they do it?" Josh was fascinated.

"I don't know, because I didn't do it." I wasn't good at lying. "I told Lenny that's what I would do if he didn't have any money. But he never gave me the chance."

Josh laughed. "It's a good thing. I don't think you would have gotten away with it."

"I might. I can put on a good act."

"You're weird. Do you put on a lot of acts?"

"No. As a matter of fact Lenny says you can see everything on my face."

Josh turned his eyes away from the road. "I don't know what you're thinking now."

"I'm thinking you'd better watch your driving."

The school dance was pretty dead. There were a million chaperons and the music wasn't terrific. I didn't want to say anything, but after a few dances — and of course no one danced with me but Josh — I said, "Do you really want to stay here?"

"No, but where can we go?"

"Jerry, Ralph's nephew, talks about a disco place. I have some money if it's expensive. Could we go there?"

"You mean Villa Maria? I don't know if

they'll let us in. They serve liquor, and I think you have to be eighteen."

"We don't have to get drinks. Maybe we can go in with someone who is eighteen. Let's try." I was in the mood to do something risky. "I'll put on more makeup and at least look like seventeen."

Josh laughed. "Maybe I could pass for eighteen, but I'd need an ID to prove it."

"I'll be back in a minute." I went to the girls' room and plastered my face as much as I could. I thought about stuffing out my blouse but decided I'd look worse.

"You don't look a day over thirty," Josh said when I got back. "Come on, Ma."

When we got to the Villa Maria we could hear the band outside. It sounded super. We decided not to try getting in on our own and chance getting turned away. So we waited until some friendly-looking people came along, to ask if we could go in with them. It was fun guessing about the people, and finally we decided on a youngish couple who looked lovey-dovey. I went up to them. "Excuse me," I said, "but my boyfriend and I are celebrating my sixteenth birthday. We're dying to go in and dance, but we think you have to be eighteen. We don't want to drink, but could you let us go in with you, please?" I looked at them with my most imploring eyes. "It would make my birthday perfect."

They looked at each other and glanced over to Josh. I guess we looked okay, and the man said, "Why not? Come on, kids, but remember, no drinking. They probably wouldn't serve you anyway. But they'll want to put us at one table." He hesitated.

"You could say the kids want to be alone, couldn't you?" I looked at him pleadingly.

"I suppose so. Come on, we'll try."

It worked terrifically, without a hitch. I kissed the lady and we thanked them both, and Josh and I had a little table in a dark corner. We drank ginger ale and danced ourselves crazy. I felt every minute that somehow I was getting back at Lenny and Liz. Don't ask me what the connection was, I don't know. I guess it was doing something Lenny would have a fit over — I mean going to a grown-up disco and lying to get in. I don't know what he thought would happen to me here. He always worried so about my not having a mother. Of course, if he thought he was about to give me one, he had another thing coming. But I didn't want to spoil this evening, so I decided to put it out of my head — just for one night.

It was about two o'clock in the morning when Josh looked at his watch and said, "Gee whiz. We'd better go home."

"Let's have one more dance."

"You're up to something tonight. What?"

I shook my head. "Nothing. Did you have a good time? Wasn't it better than the school dance?"

"Yeah, sure. But you've acted all night like

you were someplace else. I have the feeling you just wanted to stay out, and you didn't care for what."

That Josh was a perceptive kid. I had the feeling he could see into my head. "I like being with you."

Josh laughed. "You're not good at that sort of thing. You don't have to kid me. I know the real Samantha."

"Whoever she is. Never heard of her. Come on, let's dance."

It was a quarter of three when Josh let me off at my house. I let him kiss me goodnight, and thanked him for a good time, although I'd paid for half the disco. I was really hoping Lenny was having a fit waiting for me. I wanted him to be real worried. The house was dark except for a light in the hall and in a small sitting room that Lenny and I used downstairs.

The house was very quiet when I went inside. I couldn't believe Lenny had gone upstairs to bed before I came home. Maybe he'd gone to the police station to put out a search for me? I felt scared. I wanted him to be worried, but not to do anything drastic. . . . The door to the sitting room was open a little and I pushed it open further. Lenny and Liz were sitting on a small sofa in front of the fireplace, and they jumped apart when I came in. Lenny stood up. His hair was all tousled, he had his tie off and his shirt was open at the neck. The fire was burning low, perfect for roasting marsh-mallows. "Hi, Indian," he said. "Did you have a good time?"

"Very good." He hadn't even been think-ing about me. I wondered if he knew what time it was.

"How was the dance?" Liz asked. She looked tousled, too. Her hair was mussed up and she had her shoes off. Also I thought she was a little embarrassed.

"We didn't stay at the dance very long. We went to the Villa Maria, a disco place."

"You went where? The Villa Maria, that place? It has a terrible reputation. Why'd you do that?" Lenny was slowly waking up to the fact that he still had a daughter. "How'd you get in? You and Josh are too young."

"Some nice people took us in with them. We just danced. We didn't drink. The band's super."

"You had no business doing that." Lenny picked up his watch, which was lying on a table. Why did he take it off? "My God, it's almost three o'clock. For heaven's sake, Sammy, what do you think you're doing? Staying out till three o'clock, going to a disco? Are you out of your mind?"

"You didn't seem to be concerned. Not un-til this minute. I'm sorry I interrupted you." I glanced at Liz and then back at him. "I'm going up to bed."

"I'm very angry with you." Lenny was working himself up to a boil. "Staying out this late, going to a wild disco when you were supposed to be at a school dance. I won't have this kind of behavior. You're still a very young girl."

"Well, I did it. It's over and done with now. Besides, it wasn't wild." I wondered if he was putting on an act for Liz. He hadn't even known I was out so late.

"And now you're getting fresh," he said. "I've a good mind to give you a good slap."

I must have looked horrified. Lenny had never hit me in my life. "Don't you dare." I stared at him defiantly.

"I don't think he will," Liz said mildly. "Lenny's having guilt pangs. I'm afraid he didn't realize how late it was. It's my fault; I kept him talking. Come on, Lenny, do you want to drive me home?"

"Why should he feel guilty? He doesn't have to feel guilty about me. I can take care of myself." I stared at Liz coldly.

She simply smiled back. "Of course you can. But Lenny has a talent for feeling guilty. He's very good at it."

The two of them exchanged glances as if they had a secret between them. Lenny flushed. "Maybe she's right," he muttered. Suddenly he bent over and kissed me. "You know I wouldn't slap you, Indian. Go along to bed. We'll talk more tomorrow. Good night." He kissed me again, and gave me an affectionate pat on my rear end.

I undressed slowly. It had been a cuckoo evening. Josh had been right, although I hadn't wanted him to catch on, but I did want to stay out and do something wild because of Lenny. Yet coming home had been the worst anticlimax. Flat is a better word. Lenny hadn't worried about me at all. I wondered if he had asked Liz to marry him tonight. Something had happened, I was sure of that. The looks between them had been pretty heavy. I went to bed thinking I had better start making my plans.

Chapter Nine

The next day I kept waiting for Lenny to talk to me, like he said he would, but he didn't. I told myself it was because he was so busy in the restaurant, and there were a few crises like meat not getting delivered on time and the freezer going on the blink. But I began to get the feeling that whatever secret he and Liz had, they were going to keep it to themselves. The secret had to be that they were planning to get married. I didn't know what to do. I hadn't given up the thought of boarding school because I couldn't think of anything else, but I was waiting for Lenny to come out and tell me he was actually getting married.

I saw Josh a lot during vacation. Since our night at the disco, he acted like we were really going together, so I shouldn't have been surprised by what happened. Maybe I'm dumb not to have seen it coming, but I honestly wasn't prepared. Maybe if I had been, we wouldn't have had the fight.

Actually, I don't know if you would exactly call it a fight, more a disagreement, and a parting of the ways. It was at the end of our Christmas vacation. Josh and Anna and I had gone ice-skating, and after we walked Anna home, Josh came back to my house. It was on a Thursday, when the dining room was open, and although it was too early for dinner guests, the downstairs was busy, so Josh and I took hot cocoa and cookies up to my room.

I sprawled on the bed and Josh sat on the floor. All afternoon he had looked as if he was carrying a great secret, and now he kept looking at me like if he stopped looking for a minute, I'd disappear. "You keep staring at me," I said. "What's the matter? Am I growing a point on my head?"

Josh grinned. "That would be interesting. No." He dug his hand into his pocket and pulled out something wrapped in some wrinkled tissue paper. "Here, I'd like you to wear my ring. He thrust the tissue paper into my hand. "It's a signet ring I got in September when I was sixteen."

I took the ring out of the paper. It was a handsome, boy's ring with a gold band. I examined it thoughtfully.

"Put it on," Josh said.

I shook my head. "I can't take it."

"Someday you'll probably give it back to me. But I want you to wear it now. You're my girl, aren't you?"

I kept shaking my head. "No. I'm not. I can't be."

"You're not going with anyone else, are you?"

"No, but that wouldn't matter. I don't want to be anyone's girl."

Josh was getting agitated. "What are you afraid of? We see each other all the time, why can't you wear my ring?"

"Because I don't want to. I can't explain it to you. You wouldn't understand anyway."

Josh kicked my bed with his foot. "Don't tell me I wouldn't understand. How do you know what I'd understand? I'm not a ninny."

"I didn't say you were." I knew he wouldn't understand. I wasn't all clear about it myself, except for the feeling I'd had before, that if I let Josh be my boyfriend, Lenny would be pleased. And I didn't want to please Lenny. Lenny was always encouraging me to do things with Josh, or Anna, but especially Josh. Then he wouldn't have to worry about me or my being alone, I figured, and he could devote himself to Liz. It was Lenny's way of getting rid of me, telling me I needed to be with kids my age, but I wasn't going to make it easy for him. I'd get out of his way, believe me I would, but not until I was ready and I'd figured out what to do and where to go. I could just see Lenny's face if he saw me wearing Josh's ring. He'd be all smiles and bright-eyed.

"You can at least give me a reason," Josh said sulkily.

"I don't have to. We can be friends, but I'm not going to wear your ring."

Josh leaned over, took it out of my hand, and pushed it back into his pocket. He stood up. "Thanks a lot. You know what you can do. I've had enough. You're a stuck-up, spoiled kid. I don't think you care for anyone in the whole word except yourself and your precious father. I thought you really had something, but oh boy, was I wrong. I don't need you to be my friend."

"And I don't need you, either," I yelled. "You're the one who's spoiled. If you don't get what you want, you get mad. You can take your ring and stuff it. I don't need you, I don't need anybody." I rolled the tissue paper into a ball and threw it after his back as he strode out of the room.

I could hear him slam the downstairs door, and I burst into tears. I had thought he was my friend, but I had no friends. And I didn't have Lenny anymore, either. I really cried. I felt so alone. I had said I didn't need anyone, and I was determined that I didn't, but in the meantime I felt awful. I was absolutely alone. After a while I'd manage, but it was like stepping into icy cold water — you had to get used to it. I wondered how long it would take.

My marks at school weren't getting any better, and Mr. Worden asked Lenny for a conference at school. Lenny said he wanted to see Mr. Worden without me. I said I didn't care, but I hated to have people talk about me when I wasn't there. It gave me a creepy feeling.

The day Lenny went to see Mr. Worden, it had been snowing very hard. I came home to find there had been some trouble with the furnace and Lenny was down in the cellar with the furnace man. It had been a lousy day. Anna was home with a cold, and Josh walked right past me in the cafeteria and went over to sit with Candy and Peggy. I could have sat with some other kids but I sat at a table by myself. I thought I was quite dignified.

I was dying to hear what Lenny had to say, but he stayed down in the cellar for ages. Ralph was more morose than ever, predicting that the restaurant might as well close, since no one would come out in this weather. "I don't know why we bother to cook. Who will eat the food?"

"People eat, even in the snow. Maybe they'll want to get out all the more."

"By tonight it will be a blizzard," Ralph said in a dire voice, "and tomorrow morning will be ice. There will be many accidents. Mark my words."

I didn't want to mark his words. His words made me sick. When Lenny came upstairs he said he had to take a shower and get ready for the evening. "Can't you tell me what Mr. Worden said?" I cornered him in the hall.

"We'll talk about it later."

"Later you'll be busy. You're always saying later. Ralph said no one's coming out tonight."

"Ralph's a pessimist. I'd better get moving."

Later I realized Lenny had planned he wouldn't have time to talk to me. I don't mean he planned to have the furnace break down, but somehow it worked out right for him. Some guests did come to the restaurant — I think tourists on their way to skiing, who were stopped by the storm and were staying overnight in town. The restaurant was pretty busy and, surprisingly, Liz came over. I wondered why she came out in the storm, but I soon found out.

"Indian," Lenny said to me when I came down for my tray, "Liz is going to take a tray upstairs with you. Okay? She doesn't want to sit in the dining room, and the kitchen's very busy."

I didn't know what to say, but I was dumbfounded. And annoyed. I began to see Lenny's hand at work. I grunted something and heaped my plate with roast beef, potatoes, and salad. Liz followed me upstairs.

I had a small table in my room where I always ate, and where I could watch my small TV set, and I pulled over another chair for her. "This is nice and cozy," Liz said. "I hope I'm not interrupting some favorite program of yours," she said. "I love to watch TV when I eat alone, too, or read."

"There's nothing I watch right now."

"That's good, because I really want to talk to you."

My vibes were telling me to beware. I kept silent and cut up my meat.

Liz sighed. "I'm not very good at this, and I don't like it. You know your father saw your teacher today?"

"Yeah, I know. He said he'd talk to me about it later."

"He asked me to talk to you about it since it concerns me. You and me. Now, please" — she made a gesture toward me when she saw I was beginning to get angry — "I know you don't like me, and that's part of the trouble. Both your father and Mr. Worden, once he heard the whole story, are convinced you are upset about me. That's what we have to talk about."

I just looked at her and didn't say anything. She hadn't dressed up that night, but was wearing heavy boots and pants and a turtleneck sweater. She wore no makeup and she looked like a kid. Once we lived near a commune, and the young women there looked like that. I used to admire them; they looked real, the kind who didn't fuss about themselves. I had wanted to get to know them, but I never did.

"I don't know how to convince you that I'm not out to take you away from Lenny. I don't think anyone could. He loves you very much. Remember when I said he felt guilty? Well, he does. I'd like to help him get over that, but I don't want to get between you two.

127

I love him, too, Samantha, but I'd give him up if I thought I was making a rift between you two. I don't want to compete with you. Unless you can accept me, even care for me a little, no marriage between your father and me would ever work. It would be doomed from the start. I don't want to take that risk."

"That's not fair." I didn't quite yell, but I came close to it. "If you and Lenny want to get married, just leave me out of it. If you don't want to marry him, don't blame it on me. And he doesn't have to feel guilty. I'm okay. My marks aren't that bad. I won't get left back."

"You're so angry. I wish you weren't so angry. What do you know about your mother?" The sudden switch took me by surprise.

"I don't want to talk about my mother." Now I was really mad.

"I imagine you must be like her. She was a very gutsy lady."

"What do you know about my mother?"

"Only what Lenny told me. She had a lot of courage."

"What did Lenny tell you?" I was beside myself with curiosity. It got the better of my anger.

"I don't think he was able to talk about it before. He didn't say so, but I think he wanted me to tell you. That's why he talked to me."

I was still resenting that he had talked to

her, but I sat tight and listened.

"As I think you know, your mother had pneumonia, a bad case of it. Also, they had very little money, since your father was out of a job at the time." Liz adjusted herself in the chair, and although I sensed she was uncomfortable telling me all this, I kept stony-faced. I wasn't going to make it easy for her. She went on. "When Lily was getting better, Lenny asked the doctor if he couldn't take care of her at home. The hospital was costing a fortune, and besides, he had you at home to take care of. He was pretty frantic. The doctor agreed and so Lenny brought her home. But a few days later he heard about a job and he left you with a neighbor and went for an interview. It took most of the day, and when he came home your mother was delirious with a high fever. She died within a week. He felt he had failed. He was still carrying the burden of his mother's death, and then not to be able to take care of his wife — it was too much."

She looked at me then and her eyes were moist. "Your aunt didn't help, your mother's sister. She blamed him. As if he wasn't suffering enough. She even wanted to take you away, but he threw her out of the house. That's why he never hears from her. He's had a bad time, Samantha. I think that's why he's never wanted to get close to a woman before, but now if I could make him happy . . ." her voice trailed off. She stood up and walked about. "Aren't you going to say anything?"

I didn't want to see the pleading look in her eyes. "Why did he tell you?" I yelled. "You're a stranger. We hardly know you. You don't know anything about me, about us." I put my hands over my ears. "I don't want to hear about my mother from you. You're not part of our family. I wish I'd never met you. You shouldn't have listened. You should have told him to stop. He had no right to tell you, no right. . . ."

Before Liz had a chance to say anything, I got up and ran to the bathroom. I swallowed and swallowed to keep from crying, washed my face with cold water, and came back.

Liz looked at me for a minute, and then looked away. She didn't ask if I was okay. She didn't say anything for a bit. She stood up, and pushed her hair back from her face. She looked tired. "I don't know how all this is going to come out, how it is going to end. I think Lenny has brought up a splendid girl, and I'm sorry you feel the way you do. I wish I had never set eyes on either one of you. Good-night."

She picked up her tray, with her food still on the plate, and went downstairs. Something inside of me was screaming *Don't feel sorry for her — don't, don't!* Yet when I picked up a wet, crumpled Kleenex from the floor, I knew she had been crying, too. I felt awful.

Lenny came up to my room that night. It was late, but my light was still on. I guess I

knew he'd come in to see me, and I knew I
had to have it out with him, although I had
no name for my feelings. I'd been thinking
about my mother a lot, and about Lenny and
Liz — the flower lady as I thought of her
when we first met — and me. Talk about
being caught up in a web the way they say
in spooky movies. I felt completely tangled.

Lenny sat down at the foot of my bed. I
was propped up against my pillows. "Liz told
me she talked to you. I don't know if it was
smart for her to talk to you about your
mother, but I wasn't thinking of smartness.
I confess, I took an easy way out. I hadn't
talked about it to anyone before Liz, and I
had to talk to her. I hoped she'd be a help
to you, too. No matter what, your mother
would have died. Perhaps I shouldn't have
brought her home, I'll never know. I've wal-
lowed in grief and misery and guilt for too
long, honey. You don't know what Liz has
done for me. We can't lose her, she's a terrific woman, and she's going to be wonderful for both of us."

"Maybe for you. You shouldn't have told
her about my mother." I was looking down
at my blanket, not at my father. "You should
have told me. You should have told me a
long time ago. I hate that you told her first."

"I'm sorry, I'm very sorry. It probably
was the wrong thing to do, but I never could
talk about it. It's hard for me to talk about
it now. Sammy, darling, it was so awful, and
I felt such a failure. Perhaps she would have

died anyway in the hospital, I'll never know. I always thought someday, when you were older, I'd tell you about it, but with Liz it all came out. I love her, Sammy. I hope you'll forgive me."

"Then you are going to marry her?"

"If she'll have me. She has some reservations of her own." He looked at me warily. "She's very worried about you."

"She needn't be. I won't bother her. You don't have to worry about me."

"Damn it, Indian, don't give me that stuff. Of course we worry about you. And it isn't a question of you bothering her — that's a silly word. It's the way you're behaving, as if the world was coming to an end, instead of a new and wonderful life for us beginning. Can't you even try?" His face was drawn and tense and I wanted him to put his arms around me and hug me and say, "Forget everything. It's you and me, kid, the way it's always been."

"What do you want me to do?"

"I can't make you love Liz, but if you just give her a chance, I think you will of your own accord. Just stop fighting her."

"I will never love her," I said flatly. "When will you get married? Can I go to boarding school in the fall? And go someplace for the summer?"

Lenny's face darkened. "You won't give up, will you? I don't want to send you away because I'm getting married. That's a hell of a reason." He stood up. "Good night, sleep well." He went. That was the second time in my life Lenny didn't kiss me good-night.

I lay in bed luxuriating in a beautiful daydream: The restaurant was on fire — no, I didn't want that to happen, so I changed it to the nursery. Liz was trapped in the little potting room she had, and I saw the flames as I was walking by. There was no place near to call the fire engines, so I smashed the little window and dragged her out. But my hair caught on fire and soon I was up in flames. Liz was horror-stricken, and when the firemen and Lenny came she was crying over my dead body. Lenny never spoke to her again.

I went to sleep feeling much better.

Chapter Ten

I don't understand about grown-ups and how their peculiar minds work. Big, important things happen, and they pay no attention. Lenny is in love, says he wants to get married, I tell him I want to go away for the summer and then go to boarding school, and he gets all excited because the fillets of beef come in with too much fat. How can he care about anything so unimportant? It beats me. When something is on my mind, I *think* about it. Like every time I see Josh in school, in the cafeteria, or in a class, I know he's there. I can feel him looking at me when he thinks I don't know, and I think about how icky things are between us, and if he's taking Candy out now. A disagreement is not something you just forget about.

Maybe I was stupid not to take his ring. Maybe Lenny would have been jealous. But no, that was a ridiculous thought, Lenny would have been glad. I guess I was the one who was jealous, a little teeny bit, when I saw Josh having lunch with Candy so often. I might never have another boyfriend for the rest of my life, and Josh was just the kind of boy I could have fallen in love with. I wonder if there's such a thing as a second chance with someone like Josh? He's pretty fair-minded, but I'm afraid I did hurt him. It's hard to remember that anything I could do would really hurt a boy; most of them seem so sure of themselves. It's easy to think of a girl getting hurt, but not a boy.

My father hadn't said a word to me about anything since that night a few weeks ago when he came up to my room after Liz had supper with me. It's like nothing ever happened. I wish I understood what was going on. Are they going to tell me one day that they are married? Are they going to elope and leave me here with Ralph? It's very unfair of them to make a whole stir and then leave me hanging in the dark. And I'm not going to ask them, not in a million years.

January and February went by. The restaurant was pretty busy because of the skiers, and Lenny was cheerful because business was good. He and Liz saw each other a lot, but no one mentioned anything about marriage. Maybe they were waiting for spring, although somehow I didn't think Liz was the type who'd want to be a June bride.

School was boring, but for lack of anything better to do, I brought my marks up to B's and B-pluses. I even got an A for a book report. When Mr. Worden gave me my paper back with the A, he said, "I'm glad to see you doing so well. I hope whatever problems you had are being cleared up." He looked at me meaningfully.

"Nothing's any different." I saw no reason to be mysterious.

"Then you're being sensible about accepting the inevitable. That's very mature, Samantha." Okay, let him think I was mature, if, according to him, being mature was letting someone come along and ruin your whole life. I was just biding my time to see what *they* were going to do. My feelings hadn't changed. But good marks wouldn't hurt. Not if I wanted to get to boarding school, or be on my own later.

Anna and I went ice-skating a lot, and we stayed overnight at each other's houses. Lenny asked me a few times why I didn't see Josh anymore, and I told him we'd had a disagreement. "A lovers' quarrel?" he'd said with a laugh.

"Nothing of the sort," I told him. "*I* don't fall in love so easily."

He shot me a quick glance and then shook his head in a scolding way. But he didn't say anything.

After school I almost always went over to Anna's house. I really liked her mother, and it was nice to be there. I was staying out of Lenny's way as much as possible. Ever since that night we had talked there'd been a change. Lenny was Lenny, affectionate and friendly, but preoccupied. He forgot things he never used to, like on St. Valentine's day. He always used to buy me a card and a little present, but this year he didn't, and on top of that he was taking Liz out to dinner. Before he left he said, "I thought you'd get a Valentine from a real boyfriend. I thought you'd outgrown wanting one from me."

I knew he was covering up because he'd forgotten. "I haven't got a boyfriend."

"You will have one, soon enough." He gave me a kiss and hugged me. "You'll be getting tons of valentines."

"I doubt it," I told him.

He put his hand under my chin and lifted my face as if he were looking for something in it. "Don't be so downbeat, Indian." He smoothed my forehead. "I don't want to see any frowns on your pretty face."

"Have a good time," I said.

"Is Anna coming over?"

"I don't think so."

Lenny frowned. "You stay alone too much. I wish you took a little more initiative about making friends. Don't be a loner, Indian. It's no fun."

"You were for a long time. It didn't hurt you."

"I'm not so sure about that. There's a big world out there — don't turn away from it."

It was in March. A windy, blowy March night and I was having supper at Anna's. Dr. Weinstein was talking about a peace meeting he was going to. "I'm for peace," Anna said.

"We all are." Her father had a round face with twinkling eyes. "But we've got to stop the build-up of nuclear arms. We already have enough to blow up the world, and we're adding more every day. We've got to have a bilateral freeze with the Russians, that's what I'm working for. We'd better put our good minds to making better cars, instead of more missiles."

Mrs. Weinstein laughed. "You need a soapbox."

"Don't laugh, my dear. I'm a doctor, and I'm for life. Sometimes I sit in my office and think about how hard it often is to save one life, when one small nuclear bomb can kill millions."

"You're going to frighten the girls," his wife said.

"They should be frightened," he said. "That's why I'm going out to speak. So they can live happily without being frightened."

He got up to leave for his meeting before we had dessert, and Mrs. Weinstein went to see him out. "Your father's wonderful," I said to Anna. "I admire him a lot."

"He's terrific. So is your father. I guess we're both lucky."

"Mine used to be." Immediately, I felt guilty. "I shouldn't say that. He's okay, but different." Anna knew a little bit about Liz, but I hadn't talked to her much about how I felt. "Any day I expect to hear he's getting married. I wish they'd let me in on their plans."

"They'll tell you when they'll get married, won't they? Wouldn't they have a wedding?"

"I don't know. I have a feeling they'll just go off and get married. I have to find a place to go."

Anna was shocked. "You mean you'd leave?"

"You don't think I'd stay and live with them, do you?"

"Yes, I did think so. Do you hate her?"

"Not really. In a way I wish I did. But I couldn't live with someone else and Lenny. Anyway, I think he'd be glad. He wouldn't need me if he had her for a wife."

"You can have a wife and a daughter. My father has both. He just loves us differently."

"It's different for you. You've always had a mother. I haven't, so it's been different for Lenny and me."

Anna looked troubled. "I don't think you should go away."

We heard the telephone ring and her mother answered it. In a minute her mother came in and said it was for me. I was surprised. "Is it my father?"

"I don't think so," Mrs. Weinstein said.

It was Ralph. "Now don't get excited, Samantha, but your father had a little accident. I don't think it's too serious, but he's over in the hospital. I thought you'd want to go over."

My heart beat nervously. "What happened?"

"He cut his hand."

"It must be bad if he had to go to the hospital. Tell me, Ralph."

"A pretty bad cut. But he'll be all right. You go see him."

"Who took him to the hospital?"

"Miss Barnes. She rushed him right over. A good thing she was here, she knew just what to do."

I wondered what she had to do, but I flew in to get Mrs. Weinstein. "Could you drive me to the hospital? My father had an accident. He cut his hand. It must be bad if he had to go to the hospital."

"Probably he needed a few stitches. Come on, of course I'll take you."

Anna and I sat in front with Mrs. Weinstein. She got us to the hospital in less than ten minutes. "Shall we come in with you?" Mrs. Weinstein asked.

"You don't have to. My father's friend Miss Barnes is here. She brought him. I'll be okay."

"You sure?"

"Sure. As you said, he probably just needed a few stitches. I'll go to the emergency room."

"Call us later, will you?" Mrs. Weinstein leaned over and kissed me. "We'll want to know how he is."

I walked over to the emergency room entrance, and went inside, but there was no sign of Liz. I went up to a nurse at a desk. "I'm looking for Mr. Thompson. Mr. Leonard Thompson. He came in a little while ago."

"He's up in surgery. You won't be able to see him."

"He's my father. I've got to see him. Why is he in surgery?"

The nurse was looking at some charts on her desk and she wasn't very interested in Mr. Thompson or me. "I guess he needed surgery. You can go to the waiting room down there. Someone there may know. Go to the end of the corridor, turn left, and walk until you come to the elevators. One floor down." She barely looked at me.

I ran through the halls until some nurses walking by told me to slow down. It took ages for an elevator to come. Liz was there in the waiting room. She stood up when she saw me. Her face was white and drawn.

"What happened?" She put out her arms to me but I kept mine at my side.

"He had an accident." She looked at me and bit her lip. "Samantha. . . ." She was having trouble telling me. "He cut off his finger with the slicing machine." She took hold of my arm and I was afraid she was going to faint. "It was awful. . . . He lost so much blood, blood over everything."

I held her up and took her over to sit down. "He lost his finger. Oh, my God." I covered my mouth as if to keep myself from screaming. "What are they doing to him now?"

She was trying to compose herself. "They're sewing his finger back on. They have a whole team of doctors in there."

"You brought his finger with you?" The whole idea was so horrifying. I kept putting my hands over my mouth. I didn't want to ask how she'd brought it.

She nodded. And then she put her head in her hands. "We tried to stop the bleeding, Ralph and I. Ralph was wonderful. So was your father. He was in a state of shock, but he kept so calm."

"Ralph said you were wonderful, too."

She looked up and gave me a quick, grateful look. "I guess instinct takes over in a crisis. You'd better sit down." She smiled a little. "You look pretty pale yourself."

"I can't imagine anyone cutting off a whole finger. And then having it sewn back on."

"They're trying. Let's hope that it works. He's going to be in there a long time, I'm afraid. Have you eaten?"

"Yes, I ate at Anna's. Have you?"

"No, but I'm not hungry." She made a face. "I couldn't dream of eating."

He was in the operating room a long time. Hours and hours. We sat there hardly talking. Every so often one of us would get up and walk around. Once Liz went out to get some coffee. I went out to call the Weinsteins to tell them what happened. I think it was after midnight when a doctor dressed in white came into the waiting room. He turned to Liz. "Mrs. Thompson?"

"I'm not Mrs. Thompson. I'm just a friend. How is he?"

"We hope the operation will be successful. It's hard to know for a day or two if it takes, there are so many small vessels that have to be connected. They're taking him down to Intensive Care. There's always a danger of infection." He looked very tired. "If you want, you can probably see him for a minute or two. He's very groggy." He looked from her to me. "Only one of you can go in."

"This is Mr. Thompson's daughter," Liz said.

"It's up to you who sees him."

"Thank you, thank you so much for everything you've done." Liz's eyes were moist.

"We'll see. He is lucky you got him here so quickly."

Liz and I looked at each other when the doctor left us. "Go ahead," she said. "I'm sure you want to see him."

"You do, too."

She gave her funny, half smile. "Let's not argue about it. Go ahead. I saw him."

"Are you sure? You saved him."

Now she really smiled. "Don't hold that against me."

The Intensive Care unit was in another part of the building, and we went there together. Liz waited outside while I was taken in. It was weird. Lenny had a million tubes coming out of him and he was attached to all kinds of machines. His face was gray, and his hand and arm were bandaged up to the elbow. He opened his eyes and gave me a look of recognition. "Hello, Indian." He closed his eyes again. Then hardly opening them he said, "Is Liz here?"

"Yes, she is."

"Good." Speaking was an effort for him, but he had something like a smile on his face. "Tell her to stick around. I need her to pick up the parts I drop off." He gave a sigh or a grunt of satisfaction as if he had been wanting to say that for a while.

"I'll tell her." The nurse tapped me on the arm to leave.

I gave Liz his message. She laughed. "He's incredible. Never loses his humor, does he? How was he?"

"Gray and very weak. He had a million tubes in him. Do you think he's going to be all right?"

"I think so. He's very healthy. Come on, I'll take you home."

When we got to my house, Liz got out of the car with me. "I'll stay here overnight if you don't mind. I don't think you should be here alone."

"I'll be all right."

"I know you'd be all right. But I think your father wouldn't like you to be alone. Don't make a fuss." The way she looked at me, I was afraid she was going to say something mushy, but she didn't.

When we got inside I was embarrassed about where she should sleep. I didn't want her in Lenny's room, but I didn't know how to say so. There was a sofa in our downstairs sitting room, and I said I'd sleep there and she could have my bed.

"No, I'll sleep on the sofa." She insisted and didn't say anything about there being a perfectly good bed in my father's room.

When I got into bed I was very tired. But I kept thinking how peculiar it was for Liz to be sleeping downstairs, for Lenny to be in the hospital. So much had happened in just a few hours. I kept seeing Lenny's face and how awful he had looked, and then I felt panicky. What if he wasn't going to be all right? I almost wanted to run downstairs to Liz, I felt so scared. But I hung on. I forced myself to stay in bed, not to run to her. Finally, I fell asleep.

Chapter Eleven

When I woke up the next morning it took me a few minutes to remember what had happened. The sun was streaming into my window, and I thought, "It shouldn't be a beautiful, sunny day." The image of Lenny's face the night before made me want to shut out the sun — it didn't seem right for the world to go on as if nothing had happened.

I heard voices and noises downstairs, so I jumped out of bed and went down in my bathrobe. Liz was up and dressed, and Ralph and Jerry were there. They were sitting around the kitchen table, and Liz had a pad and pencil in her hand.

"You say Lenny had ordered the chickens and they were to be picked up this morning? Why can't they be delivered?" Liz was addressing Ralph.

"Mr. Thompson gets them right from the farm. He likes to pick out the ones he wants. He's fussy about the breasts. Maybe Jerry can get them."

"No, I can go. You'll need Jerry here. What else had you planned for tonight?"

"We have everything — the veal, a beef stew that is already made ... the only thing is fish. Maybe we don't need fish on the menu tonight."

Liz saw me standing in the doorway. "Good morning, Sammy. Aren't you late for school?"

"I'm not going. I want to go to the hospital to see my father."

"I'm not sure you'll be able to see him, but of course go, by all means. I don't suppose it will hurt you to miss school for a day."

I had expected an argument, but she gave me her bright smile instead. "Come and have some breakfast," she said.

"What's going on here?" I poured myself a glass of orange juice and took out my box of cereal.

"We're planning for tonight, for the restaurant."

"Are you going to run the restaurant?" I looked at her warily.

"I'm going to help. I think together we can do it."

"Did my father tell you to?"

Liz frowned. She looked annoyed, but just for a second. "No, your father was not up to telling anyone anything. I'm doing it on my own, Sammy. I rather think he'd be pleased."

"I don't know." I spoke slowly, carefully pouring milk into my cereal bowl. "He's awfully fussy about this place. Maybe he'd rather have it closed for a couple of weeks, until he comes back. He may not be in the hospital for long."

"We can do it okay," Ralph said. "Miss Barnes is a smart lady, and I've watched your father. Maybe I won't do as good, but it won't be bad. For a little while we can manage. It is not good to close a restaurant, people go other places and don't always come back."

"I think we should wait and ask him. Maybe he can talk to me today." To have Liz come in and run things was more than I could bear. She was wriggling her way into our lives, and now there'd be no way to get her out. This was just the kind of thing Lenny would fall for, he'd think it was marvelous that she kept the restaurant going while he was in the hospital. He wouldn't see how pushy she was — he of all people who hated pushy women — and how she was just trying to hook him.

"I am doing this on my own," Liz said, her eyes stormy. It was the closest to being angry I'd ever seen her. "I take full responsibility for it, Samantha."

I was angry, too. This was it. I could see her taking over Lenny, pushing me out. All my pent up resentment, hurt, and anger came pouring out. I couldn't have held it back if I'd wanted to. Underneath, my worry about Lenny was driving me to the edge. "This is my house," I said. "Lenny is my father, and

148

I don't want anyone running the restaurant unless he says so." We stared coldly at each other.

Liz stood up. "Yes, this is your house, I can see that. If you're telling me to leave, you'll have to say so." Her dark blue eyes were flashing and her face was flushed.

"I don't care whether you stay or go, but you're not going to run the restaurant."

"Okay, I'm going. I have no desire to stay here with you. I happen to care about your father, I care for him very much, but how in the world he managed to have a spoiled, possessive child like you, I don't know. I feel sorry for you. You are doing everything you can to ruin your father's life, and I can only hope you don't succeed." She stormed out of the room and out of the house.

I stared at Ralph and Jerry for a moment, and then ran upstairs to my room. I was horrified by what had happened. I hadn't meant for her to go like that, I had just wanted to wait and ask Lenny. I didn't like for her to take for granted that she could take over, as if she was part of our family already. Now I was scared, terrified. I didn't know what to do. I hadn't meant to really break up things between Lenny and her, but I didn't want to be ignored, to be left out. Why hadn't she asked me if it was all right for her to run the restaurant? I was a person. She had acted as if I didn't exist. I wasn't a baby, she could have asked me, Lenny always did. Her words had hurt. Was I a spoiled, possessive child? I didn't want to spoil Lenny's life, I didn't want to keep him from being happy. I wished I had died with my mother, or never been born. Lenny should have given me away to an orphanage instead of bringing me up to love him so much.

When I went downstairs, Ralph was in the kitchen alone. "Where's Jerry?" I asked him.

"He went for the chickens," Ralph said morosely.

"Are you going to have the dining room open tonight?"

"Yes." Then he looked at me with his mournful eyes. "If it's all right with you?" He was almost smiling. "Maybe not such a full menu like your father has, but enough."

"That will be wonderful. Ralph, what should I do? I didn't mean for her to go away. I got mad. And I don't know why, it just happened."

"Maybe you should go and apologize. Miss Barnes is a fine lady. Your father likes her very much."

"I know." I sighed. To go and apologize . . . I wasn't sure I could do that. "Ralph, can you drive me to the hospital?"

"I suppose so. But how will you get back? I have a lot of work to do here."

"I don't know, I'll manage. I can hitch a ride. Just take me. I've got to see my father."

They had moved him out of Intensive Care and into a private room. I couldn't believe it. He looked almost like Lenny, not like that gray, almost-dead person he'd been after the operation. He was propped up against the pillows, but when I bent over to kiss him and saw him closer, I could see he still wasn't his usual self. His face was drawn and his voice was weak. "Hello, Indian," he said cheerfully. "Your father made quite a fool of himself. I always pride myself on being so careful — for me to do a dumb thing like that . . . Don't know how it happened. Good thing Liz was there to pick up the pieces. Don't know how she had the presence of mind to save my finger. I was bleeding like a pig; most women would have fainted. Wonder where she is. Thought she'd be here by now."

"Maybe she's not coming." I pulled up a chair close to his bed.

Lenny looked alarmed. "She all right?"

"Yes, I guess so. I had a fight with her. Lenny, I feel awful. I didn't mean to, but she got mad and I got mad, and she stormed out of the house. She hates me."

Lenny looked more ashen than before. "I'm afraid you're the one who hates her." His voice was very tired. "Okay. I guess it had to happen sooner or later. It was nice while it lasted, but if you hate her, it wouldn't work. I suppose it's better to end it now than later."

"You mean you're just going to let her go, like that?" My heart was beating nervously.

"What else can I do? I'm not blaming you, Sammy. If you don't like her, you don't. I couldn't marry someone you hated so much. The marriage wouldn't work, that's all. You're my daughter and I promised your mother I'd take care of you, and I have. I'm not about to make you miserable now. No woman in the world is more important to me than you are."

"But Lenny, I . . . I feel awful. . . ." I burst into tears. "I don't really hate her," I sobbed. "She just doesn't understand about you and me. You've never made me feel like a baby, you made me feel important. To her I'm just another kid. She came in today to run the restaurant for you, she never asked me, she acted like I was nobody. . . ."

"She was going to run the restaurant?" Lenny perked up. "How about that? She doesn't know a damn thing about a restaurant, but I bet she'd do a bang-up job. Imagine her wanting to do that. She's terrific."

"But she's not going to do it." I was still sobbing. "I stopped her. That's what we had the fight about. I wanted her to ask you first, and she got mad. Then I got mad, and she left."

"Is the restaurant going to be closed?"

"No, Ralph's doing it. With Jerry."

Lenny frowned. "Ralph can do some foolish things. He doesn't know how to order. Liz would be better at that." He looked worried. "Do you think she'd like me to call her?"

"I don't know. She said she cared about

you." I looked away from him. "But she said some pretty mean things to me. She said I was a spoiled, possessive child."

"Did she say that?" Lenny's frown deepened, and then he laughed. "She must have been angry. Don't take it to heart. Maybe we'd better show her that you're not. Probably my fault if you are. Why don't you go over and apologize to her? How about that?"

"That's what Ralph told me to do."

"So?" He looked at me questioningly.

"I'll think about it. What are you going to do?"

"I'll have to think about it, Indian. I guess I don't really want it to be the end. I haven't loved another woman since your mother, but, well, Liz is important to me. I keep thinking that if you two really got to know each other, you'd hit it off beautifully. Maybe I've been in too much of a hurry. Give me some time to figure things out, but don't be too hard on Liz. You and I have had something special going and it's not easy for someone else to break in. Let's not make any big decisions now." He held out his good hand and gave mine a squeeze. "I hope you'll go see her." He looked at me in a way that made me know a lot depended on what I would do. His eyes had a searching, pleading quality that asked me, more than any words, to make up with Liz.

"What do you want me to bring you from home?" I wanted to leave.

Lenny gave me a list including pajamas,

shaving stuff, some papers he wanted, a few books, and some decent food when they'd let him eat it. "I don't know how long they're going to keep me here. I guess they have to see how my finger is healing. Quite a job they did. Imagine sewing my finger back on. Hope they were good seamstresses."

I didn't tell Lenny I was going to hitch a ride home, and thank goodness he didn't think to ask me how I was going. Right outside the hospital I got a ride with a lady who was going not far from our house. At the house, Ralph had gotten Lena and Mary to come in early, and the kitchen was busy with all of them working.

"What can I do?" I asked Ralph.

"Nothing right now. Too bad you can't drive, you could do some errands. Miss Barnes could have done them." He gave me a sorrowful look. "How is your father?"

I told him, and then went upstairs to make a pile of the things Lenny wanted. I figured I'd take them to the hospital later in the afternoon.

After I collected Lenny's stuff, I sat down in my room to try to sort things out in my head. I knew I should go over to apologize to Liz, but I had to think about it a lot. If I went it would mean that she and Lenny would get married. I was sure of that. But if I didn't, maybe Lenny would forget about her, and that would be the end of it.

But how could he forget about her when

she lived just down the road? If only he
didn't have the restaurant and we could move
away. I was scared. I didn't want to be the
one to decide our life, I shouldn't be the one
to decide if Lenny should get married. And
yet, wasn't that exactly what I did want?

I felt that whatever I did, this was the
most important moment in my life. A turning point. I thought of all the things people
had said to me — "You and your father are
too close"; "You'll never find anyone to treat
you the way your father does" — and Liz
saying I was spoiled and possessive. I didn't
want to be. And yet Lenny and I were close.
We couldn't undo that.

I was still in my room thinking, when I
heard voices downstairs. I went down to see
who was there, and it was Anna and Josh.
Josh looked a little embarrassed, and Anna
ran over to me with a hug and a kiss. "I'm
sorry about your father. Josh thought you
might need someone to drive you and he has
his mother's car. What can we do?"

"Oh, Anna." I almost bawled. "I don't
know what there's to do. You're so wonderful to come over." I looked from her to Josh.
For Josh to come now, after we hadn't been
seeing each other, made me feel weepy. If
Anna hadn't been there I would have hugged
him.

"We're your friends," Josh said.

I'd never had close friends like this before.
It was tremendous. "I'll see if Ralph needs

anything. Then maybe you could take me back to the hospital. My father asked me to bring him a few things."

"Of course. That's what we're here for." They both spoke at once.

Ralph gave me a small list of things he needed, and the three of us drove off. Josh and Anna waited downstairs while I went up to see Lenny. He looked more tired than he had in the morning. "Did you go to see Liz?" he asked.

"Not yet."

"Are you going to go?" He held my eyes. He looked sad, not like Lenny.

"I'm going to try."

"I've been thinking of your mother. She'd have liked Liz. Your mother had plans of going back to school when you were older. She never even finished high school, but she wanted to study designing. She wanted to be a fashion designer. Did you know that?"

"No. You've never told me much about my mother. You never wanted to talk about her. I only know she could sew."

"I never could talk about her. It wasn't fair to you, I realize that. Liz opened up that box, and it's a good thing. I was carrying around a baggage of guilt I didn't need. You can at least be grateful to Liz for that."

"I suppose so."

Lenny laughed at the way I said it. "You begrudge Liz everything."

"Maybe I've got to get used to the idea. It's kind of like a bomb was dropped."

Lenny threw me a sharp glance. "It's been that way for me too, Indian. I never thought I'd fall in love this way."

"You love her a lot?"

He nodded his head. "Yes, I do. But it doesn't take away from loving you." He laughed again. "I've got room for you both."

Lenny looked very tired, so I left. We got the things for Ralph, and then Josh and Anna took me home. "We'll come around tomorrow," Anna said, "and see if you need anything."

"Thank you, that's terrific."

Later, Josh called me up. We just chatted about nothing in particular. He didn't say anything about our fight and neither did I. But I was very glad he had called.

Chapter Twelve

The next morning I knew would be the key day: Either I'd see Liz that day or I never would. I ate breakfast nervously. It was Saturday, no school, and Ralph and Jerry had come in early again. The night before the dining room had gone okay. It wasn't too crowded, but they expected more people Saturday night. Everyone seemed nervous. Ralph was pounding veal and swearing.

"You shouldn't talk that way," Jerry said. "There's a lady present."

Ralph grunted. "She ain't no lady, she's a kid."

"I'm a lady kid," I told him. I laughed. "A goat."

Jerry giggled. "A nanny goat, that's what you are."

We were all nervous and silly.

I made my breakfast last as long as I could. I took a second helping of cereal, which I didn't want, and threw most of it away when Ralph wasn't looking. He was very heavy about wasting food.

"I'm going out for a walk," I said to Ralph after breakfast.

I walked up the hill slowly. I stopped at the cemetery and read some of the gravestones. But that was too spooky, so I didn't do that for long.

I went past the nursery but I didn't see Liz outside. I decided that was a sign, although I didn't know what she'd be doing outdoors on such a cold day. When I walked back again I saw her in the greenhouse. She glanced up once and I think she saw me, but I wasn't sure.

Finally I went up to the greenhouse and went inside. She greeted me as usual. "Hello, Samantha. It's pretty cold out there, isn't it?"

"Yes, very."

She went on with what she was doing, taking care of her plants.

"I came to apologize," I said. "I'm sorry I was rude."

She looked up at me. The sun was shining in, and her eyes were very blue. She always had some tan, even now, in the winter. "Are you? Well, I'm glad you came over."

Somehow I had expected her to say more. Now it seemed that she expected me to leave. "I told my father what happened. I think he'd like you to come visit him."

She smiled a little. "I suppose he would. But I think it would be foolish, don't you?"

159

"Oh, no. I don't think so. I think you should."

"No, I think not. It was nice of you to apologize, but it really doesn't change anything, does it? Feelings don't change that easily. The way you feel about me is still the same."

"But yours and Dad's feelings, they must still be the same, too, aren't they?"

"For a while probably. Eventually we'll get over it." She watered some tiny, baby plants, pouring the water very carefully.

"Lenny will be miserable. He loves you a lot."

"I love him, too."

"Then why won't you go to see him?"

"You know why." She looked up at me. "Let's not fool each other, Samantha. You're a nice girl. When I said you were spoiled I meant only where Lenny is concerned, and I don't think that's your fault. But I think it would be impossible for any woman to marry Lenny and live with him happily. Maybe later, when you are married yourself. But now you would come between them whether you wanted to or not."

"But that's awful. I don't want to, honestly I don't. I don't want to ruin Lenny's life. Please, give me another chance."

Liz studied my face, but hers was dubious. Her mouth trembled. "Don't think I don't want to see him. I can't bear not seeing him, especially now when he's in the hospital. It's awful. I haven't slept for two nights."

She wasn't cool and collected Liz anymore, and suddenly I felt sorry for her. I was tempted to put my arms around her, but I felt silly about doing it. "Please go to see him."

"I'll think about it," she said.

When I got home, Josh was waiting for me. "You want a ride to the hospital?"

"Sure."

When we were in the car, I said, "It's terrific of you to take me. And of your mother to let you have the car."

"On the weekend my Dad's home, and they use his car. Anyway, like Anna said, we're your friends."

"I know. I'm in a mess about my father and Liz." I poured out the story to Josh. He wasn't surprised because he knew enough about the three of us. "I make a mess of my relationships, don't I?" Our eyes met and he knew I was thinking about the two of us, Josh and me. "It means a lot to me that you came over with Anna when my father went to the hospital. You've been terrific, Josh. I'm not very good at apologizing."

"That's okay, you don't have to." He was embarrassed, but I was glad I'd said what I did. "What should I do?" I asked, coming back to my father and Liz.

"Just what you did. I think she'll go see him. I don't know what more you can do."

"I don't either. Except — Josh, I wish I

knew how I felt. I mean if they do get married, I may really be miserable."

"Or maybe you won't. I was awfully mad at you about my ring. I thought I hated you. But I don't. You don't have the same feelings forever. You want to be friends, we can be friends. We don't have to be boy-girl friends, if you know what I mean."

"Oh." I paused a moment. It hadn't occurred to me that Josh would give up so gracefully. Josh looked at my expression and laughed. "There's always a chance you'll change your mind." I laughed, too.

I didn't tell my father I'd gone to see Liz. I wanted him to be surprised if she came. He looked a little better, but I didn't stay long because the doctors came in.

When we left the hospital, Josh asked if I wanted to ride over to an art gallery with him. His father had a couple of photographs on exhibit. His father was an accountant, but photography was his hobby. I said okay. I was glad to have something to do. Ralph had said he didn't need me.

The gallery was fun. There were some weird pictures of frogs and insects, all blown up, and they looked real crazy. Josh's father's pictures were good, especially one of an old couple sitting on a bench in a park. They looked a million years old, but content, with the sun shining on them. The other picture was a shadowy doorway with a girl standing in it. "Who is she?" I asked Josh.

"A friend of my mother's. The daughter

of a friend. My father likes to take pictures of her."

"She's pretty." I glanced up at Josh.

"If you're asking do I like her, yes. But she's twenty-six years old. A little old for me." He laughed. "Don't tell me you're jealous?"

"What if I were? But I'm not the jealous type," I added hastily.

"That's what you think. You're jealous of your father."

"I love him."

"That's what makes people jealous, dope. If you didn't care, you wouldn't be jealous. I'm sorry you're not jealous of me."

"That doesn't mean I don't like you. Besides, don't be so sure."

"Wow. I can't believe it. You actually said something nice."

"Am I really so awful?" I turned to him, honestly concerned.

"You don't hand out compliments easily." He grinned. "But that's okay if you save them for me."

When Josh took me home he said he was trying to get a group together to play, and a few guys were coming over to his house that night to practice. "Some girls, too. Will you come?"

"Sure," I told him. "How will I get there?"

"I'll come pick you up, around eight?"

I had just washed my hair, and was putting polish on my nails, when I heard Liz's voice downstairs. I don't know what made me think of it, but I remembered the first day Lenny took me to see the restaurant. I had put green polish on my toenails. It seemed a hundred years ago. "Can I come up?" Liz called.

"Yeah, sure."

Her face was flushed. Rosy from the cold, I thought, but maybe more than that. I led her into my bedroom. "I went to see your father," she said, and sat down on the chair by my desk. I sat on the bed.

"Your father wants us to get married as soon as we can. He insisted that I tell you, I thought he should, but he said he wouldn't see you till tomorrow, and he wanted you to know right away. You know your father, he likes to do everything in a hurry."

"Yes, I know." Only that morning he'd said maybe he had rushed things, and now this. Wow! I didn't know what to feel or what to say. I couldn't say I was surprised, because I wasn't. I knew it was going to happen. I'd known it for a long time. Now, it was almost an anticlimax. I couldn't wonder about it any more, and I couldn't fight it. For a while I didn't feel anything. I should have kissed her, or done something, but I just sat there like a dope.

"Aren't you going to say anything?" Liz asked quietly.

"I don't know what to say." I looked up at her. "I knew it was going to happen, but

I still have to get used to the idea."

"Are you terribly upset?"

"No, I don't think I am. It seems peculiar, but also natural in a way. I — I'm going over to Josh's tonight. Not a real party, just some kids playing some music." Suddenly I wanted to talk about myself. I didn't want to think about them. "What do you think I should wear?"

"Let's see what you've got." Liz walked over to my closet. It was a mess, jammed with stuff, some of it on the floor. But she didn't say anything about that. She looked at my clothes, at least what she could see. She pulled out a pleated, plaid wool skirt. "This looks nice. Have you got a top that goes with it? It looks warm, too."

"Yes, I've got a navy blue pullover. I could wear that with dark wool kneesocks. Do you think that would be all right?"

"I think it would be fine. Have a good time. Your father asked me to stay and help Ralph tonight. He spoke to Ralph on the phone, and he expects a busy evening."

Her eyes caught mine and I gave an embarrassed laugh. "I'm glad you can help him," I said.

"Have you got a ride to Josh's?"

"Yes, he said he'd pick me up. He'll bring me home, too."

I had a super time at Josh's. His parents were really neat. They weren't the kind that came nosing around, but around ten-thirty or eleven, his mother brought out some terrific food, and we all stuffed ourselves. The boys played well. Even Anna, who once said she only liked classical music, thought it was good.

It was after twelve when Josh drove me home. We sat in the car for a few minutes talking. I told him Liz and my father were going to get married. "Do you mind terribly?" he asked.

"I'm not sure. I don't know. Ask me a year from now. If I hate living with them, I'll go away to boarding school. I'll have to see."

"Do you always do what you want?" I didn't know whether he was criticizing me or complimenting me.

"No, but I try. What's wrong with that?"

"Nothing. At least you know what you want."

"Sometimes, not always. I know now I'd better go in."

Josh leaned over and kissed me. "You're a terrific girl."

"Thank you." We kissed again, and I really liked it. I hugged him hard and he kissed me hard and I kissed him back the same way. Josh laughed. "Wow. When you do something you really do it."

I was embarrassed. "Did I do something wrong? I'm not very experienced." I didn't tell him I'd never kissed anyone like that before.

"No, you didn't do anything wrong. Just don't go around doing that to everyone."

"I wouldn't to anyone but you." We kissed good-night again, and I ran into the house.

I was surprised to find Liz in the kitchen. She was having a cup of tea. "I hope you don't mind that I waited for you."

"No, that's okay. How did everything go tonight?" I hadn't thought about the restaurant or Lenny all evening. I couldn't believe it.

"Everything was fine. One customer sent the veal back because it was pink, but that's the way it should be. Did you have a good time?"

"Yes. Super. Liz, what's it like to be in love?"

"It's marvelous. You feel so alive, everything is suddenly sharper and clearer. You wake up remembering something terrific has happened to you, and you go to sleep thinking about it. And all day it's there, like having a beautiful, lovely secret. There's nothing like it."

"I hope I fall in love someday. You said I never would. But I think I will. I'd like to feel that way."

"I think you will. You're changing already, Samantha. You're going to be a lovely woman. I'm glad I'm going to be around to watch you grow."

I remembered that when I first met her I wanted to be like her, and suddenly I thought, *Gee whiz, she can help me.* But she wasn't mushy, and I wasn't going to be. We said good-night, and she went home and I went up to bed.

I fell asleep thinking of how Josh and I had kissed. It wasn't until the next morning that I remembered I hadn't asked Liz last night how my father was.

About the Author

Hila Colman grew up in New York City and was graduated from Radcliffe College. After college, she did publicity and promotion work; then she wrote articles for magazines and eventually she began to write books. She has been writing books for teenagers for many years. "I love teenagers," she says, "I am on their side because they are fluid, fermenting, and rich with life and living."

She lives in Bridgewater, Connecticut, where she is very active in the town's government. She is the author of *Sometimes I Don't Love My Mother* and *Girl Meets Boy*.